THE
NEXT
BEST
THING

LITTLESHIRLY

Copyright © 2024 LITTLESHIRLY.

All rights reserved. No part of this book may be reproduced, stored, or transmitted by any means—whether auditory, graphic, mechanical, or electronic—without written permission of both publisher and author, except in the case of brief excerpts used in critical articles and reviews. Unauthorized reproduction of any part of this work is illegal and is punishable by law.

ISBN: 979-8-89031-828-2 (sc)
ISBN: 979-8-89031-829-9 (hc)
ISBN: 979-8-89031-830-5 (e)

Because of the dynamic nature of the Internet, any web addresses or links contained in this book may have changed since publication and may no longer be valid. The views expressed in this work are solely those of the author and do not necessarily reflect the views of the publisher, and the publisher hereby disclaims any responsibility for them.

One Galleria Blvd., Suite 1900, Metairie, LA 70001
(504) 702-6708

You never know what the day is going to bring and what you might get into during the course of it. But, what I do know is that in life you should expect the unexpected, that way the shock of whatever happens won't kill you. My name is Simone McKnight and this is my story of confusion.

See, I'm a smart young thirty one year old woman. I live alone in a loft apartment near the southern burbs. I work for a government contracted company called Blue Steel. I'm a biochemist. I went to school at the University Of Pennsylvania, Philadelphia, my home state and town. I lived at home with mom and dad while I was in school. Because of my demanding schedule with working and school, it all paid off in the end. I develop fuels, medications, and many other things I'm not supposed to tell you about, or I'll have to kill you. Anyway, I'm the youngest on the staff and tend to be a work-a-holic. I stumbled across a new form of synthetic fuel to use in military fighter jets that is cheaper to make, burns longer, and cleaner. They are still testing it but it looks promising, and if it goes through I'll be up for promotion. I love my job. It's hard work but like I said before, it's all worth it. Even though I'm far from home I still have made a lot of friends, and I always call and go home on the important holidays. I have a good career in the field of my choice, in the area of my choice. I have a good grip on my life, or at least I thought. Things always seem to happen just when you think you have everything under control, and your life is moving at just the right speed. My best friend in the world, she was the only person that could make me laugh like she did, so it was a treat to get away with her. Her name is Louise Hathaway, I called her Weezy for short. Weezy was a psychiatrist, and a well known one at that. I met Weezy in the gym of our apartment building in the sauna. This busted up looking woman had come into the sauna, and not only did she look like hell on wheels, she smelled like it too. You know, the only thing you do in a sauna is sweat. After being smothered by the odor for about five minutes Louise got up and left 'cause the lady was sitting next to her, so she smelled it before I did. Not long after though, the funk had floated its ass right past my nose and that's when I had to roll out. I was in the locker room getting my bag together to go upstairs and shower, when Louise had come to her locker after being in the showers, and I'm a people person, so I spoke. "That lady was wrong for coming in there smelling like that." Louise looked at me and fell out laughing. "I have never smelled anything like that before in my life, and she sat her shitty ass right next to me!" I fell out laughing then. We talked about that damn lady so bad we wanted to go right to church and pray for ourselves 'cause we knew we were going to hell. From that day forth we were like white on rice. She had been living here in Atlanta longer than I had been, but she moved in the building not long after I did. I'm saving to buy a house but this place was good for now. Weezy made good money and she saved as well. She was good with money, and stocks, and all that other electronic-internet money shit. She had made us quite a bit of money in the past few years. Because of her I was able to buy a brand new Bentley, and I'm going to be able to buy my dream house a lot sooner than I thought. I'm pretty settled in here though, but I'm going to save that house money. Weezy treated lots of people, and was in the paper quite a few times 'cause she got some of the best reviews in the city. She also wrote a book called, *What Gets On The Brain's*

Nerves. It sold over a million copies and was on Oprah's book of the month list. Weezy had style. She was classic and crazy, some of my favorite traits. Neither of us had much luck with men for the simple fact that a lot of men are intimidated by an intelligent woman, and the ones that have the guts to say something think they're players or God's gift to women, that they can have any woman they want. I was in a relationship for two and a half years, and we were engaged to be married. His name was Blair Armstrong. Believe me that man's arm WAS STRONG, and I'm not talking about the ones attached to his shoulders. When he made love to me I felt like I was flying. I loved him more than I loved myself. I moved my soul out and moved his in. He had a caramel vanilla complexion, with dark curly hair. He was half Jamaican and half Puerto Rican. That man was fine. His lips were full and juicy like navel orange slices and twice as sweet. He was strong, funny, smart, and spoke with that thick Jamaican accent, in a deep voice that just made my panties moist. I did whatever that man asked me to do, and he never had to ask twice. He owned his own construction company called High Rise. They worked on and built large structures. I love a man who is good with his hands. His body was chiseled from stone, and tight with skin as soft as butter. He put those lips any and everywhere he could, when he could. He would cook and clean, and was no stranger to hard work. He would always say, "My mama didn't raise a bum." I met him in a Reggae club under the thick cloud of purple haze that loomed over me. I was dancing to Beres Hammond's, Come Back Home, and I turned to see the most beautiful man I had ever seen in life walking in my direction. He walked right up to me and asked me to dance. I was speechless and just nodded my head in acceptance. He smelled wonderful. He was wearing an oil that seemed to hypnotize me. It had a light smell of musk, cider, and citrus, very strong, but not overbearing. He held me close, and he held me tight. I drifted into a place I didn't want to return from. I felt like a little girl being romanced for the first time. He had on a pair of baggy jeans with a rhinestone design on one of the legs, and a black wife beater with a rhinestone design on it as well. He was wearing a black bandana tied around his head so that his curls exploded from the top like a volcano. I could see every muscle in his arms. While we danced I held on to him as if he were superman, and just saved me from the world. After the dance he took my hand and led me out the front door. "My name is Blair", he said and the sound of his thick Jamaican accented deep baritone voice shook me to my soul, and I could've sworn I had an orgasm right there. I still couldn't speak. He saw how in awe I was of him and he kissed my cheek. He lit a fire between my legs I wasn't going to be able to put out by myself no matter how hard I tried. "My name is Simone," I finally said. "It's nice to meet you, Simone." He replied. "Would you like to get a cup of coffee or tea so we can talk?" The yes I answered fell out my mouth like a fat bitches titty out of a too small bra. "Do you want to ride in my car, or do you want to follow me?" I don't know this dude. "I'll follow." I said. "Well, I'll walk you to your car. Don't move until I pull up okay." I nodded. He walked me to my car, and when he walked to go get his car, he kept turning around as if I were going to disappear and he could keep an eye on me so that wouldn't happen. He pulled up in his car and I followed him to this little café on this little block in Center City, Philadelphia. We were on our way in when he grabbed my arm, and stopped me from opening the door. He pulled me close and we began to dance to the Nina Simone they had playing on a speaker in front of the store. I would have sold my soul to stay in that moment forever knowing what I know now. After the song played, I didn't want coffee anymore and neither did he. He stared into my eyes and kissed my lips. I couldn't stop him. I didn't want to. He took my hand once more and we began to walk without speaking. Before I knew it we were in an elevator, then in a hallway, then in his bedroom. He lit one candle and sat it on top of his Italian wood chest that sat in front of a king size bed, neatly made, and dressed in a wine and black colored sheet set and comforter. A bed fit for a king. Everything about this room said a man lived here. His cologne filled the air and I almost lost myself. The room was neat but lived in, and everything seemed to be large. You know, just for him. The mahogany furnishings gave off a small sweet wooded scent that was intoxicating, and it made the hair on the back of my neck stand up. There was no carpet, and the three-wick candle light danced on the well-polished floor. He moved some things off his dresser and placed the candle there. He picked up a remote and music began to play. Amanda Perez began to sing, "You Make Me Feel", and feel him I did. I felt him before he laid a hand on me. I felt him in places quiet, soft and moist, that were now going to become loud, raw and satisfied. He walked over to me slowly, as if to not frighten me. Neither of us made a sound but we both understood the conversation we were having without words. He stood in front of me tall like a redwood. He was six feet two inches, and two hundred ninety four pounds of pure man. I looked up at him and I traced his body from his head to his toes, then brought my eyes back to his chest that seemed like it could block the sun. I felt a little ashamed 'cause I was about to sleep with a man I had only met hours before, but I needed this, I needed him. With school and work I never got a break, so when I did get time off I just wanted to relax. The only reason I went out was because finals were over and I had off that weekend, and 'cause my girlfriend, Tina, had dragged me out. Tina and I were in the same math class, and she was cool so we went out some times. She was going to be mad when she realized that I left the club but she drove there too, so she wasn't stranded. This man standing in front of me was the answer to all my prayers, even if just for the night. As he stood in front of me I knew I was in the presence of one of God's greatest creations, and all I could do was submit to his every whim. He lifted one of those big hands and rubbed my forehead; down my cheek, across my neck, between my breasts, to my belly button where he stuck his finger in the skirt I was wearing, and let his finger dance against the short pubic hair it reached. I had on a white

Enyce cotton pleated skirt and tank top set that complimented everything about my almond milk chocolate complexion. The tank was lined with red and blue, as well as the waist of the skirt. On my feet I wore a pair of white Tommy Hilfigure sneakers trimmed in blue and red as well, which he gently slid off my feet as I braced myself on him while his face was now level with the place below my hips, that at this point I wanted him to touch the most. I placed my hand on his back and he felt so solid, almost in-destructible. As he stood up, he ran his hand up my calf, and up my thigh until his fingertips met with the white cotton thong I was wearing. The guitar on the record that was playing put me at a state of ease and then Amanda Perez said, "You make me feel like I need to be loving you, holding you, feeling you next to me. You make me so secure; your love is so pure. It makes me feel like I need more. You make me feel so safe. I couldn't never let no one come and take your place. You make me feel. You make me feel." His finger followed the trail laid out by the thong down to the front where he noticed, if hadn't before, that I was extremely aroused from the fluid that was now starting to run down my leg. He removed one hand to find the shiny substance on his fingertips and to my surprise he put them in his mouth. I wanted him so bad my groin began to ache with anticipation. He then stuck both hands in the thong with his fingers spread so while he removed them he could grip my voluptuous ass in his big hands. He touched me as gently, as you would a blind virgin. He looked deep into my eyes through it all. His big brown eyes felt warm, like a lit fireplace in winter. He lifted the tank top over my head and removed my bra so that now all the clothing remaining on my body was my skirt and socks. He bent over and tasted my nipple, which had long been awaiting some attention. His tongue to my skin weakened me. He knew what he was doing to me. He knew what he was making me feel. I was clay for his hands to now mold. Tonight I was going to give him more than I had ever given anyone, even myself. He then slowly slid the skirt off, and I was naked. Even thought it was just he and I, I felt like I was standing in a room with one hundred people in it with all eyes on me. He stepped back and looked at me as if he were admiring a piece of art. Him, still being dressed except for his shoes, pulled my naked body toward him and he kissed me. That kiss melted my whole past away, and now all I could see was him in my future. His lips were as soft as silk in the sun. My body temperature seemed to rise five degrees. He was a very big man, but he was very gentle. Neither of us spoke the whole time except for the occasional moan, most of them coming from me when his fingers ventured into those soft and quiet places on my body. I felt like a virgin. Now, this wasn't my first time around the block. I had had a boyfriend or two, and I knew quite a few tricks to the trade, but this Blair seemed to kill all my defenses, and no it wasn't the weed. I couldn't dismiss him like so many before. He placed my hands on his chest still standing two inches in front of me. I didn't know what to do. I felt like I was given a million dollars and didn't know what to buy first. It was clear that he wanted me to undress him, so I did. I undid his belt and freed his shirt from the confines of his jeans. I just laid my face to his chest in the soft hair that lightly coated it. I rubbed his nipples and his rock hard stomach, and kissed him all over it gently. He was so beautiful, a life-like statue. I rubbed his arms for which I imagined them keeping me safe from the world. My face never left his chest. I rubbed my face on his chest much like a cat does to show affection, or when they find a comfortable place. I pressed my body against his as I rubbed and ran my hands up his world holding back and then up his chest, past my face, to his burden caring shoulders. His smell just made me want to eat him. As my body was pressed up against his, I could feel his excitement. My face parted with his chest and I stepped back to remove his jeans. I too put both hands in, palms in, so I could feel his huge thighs as the jeans were released from their fixed position. Once they passed his taut ass they fell to the floor. He then just stepped out of them. His manhood looked like a mad dog waiting to come out of a cage that had a raw piece of meat hanging in front of it. He wore boxer briefs, my favorite. They were charcoal colored Calvin Klein's. I grabbed them and looked at him as I worked them off his big body, and his dick jumped out like a man leaping for his life from a plane. I looked down and the size of it made my lips separate. I looked back up at him, and he was still looking at me. He knew I would be pleased. We were now naked. He stepped to me and picked me up under my arms like you would a child. I weigh one hundred fifty five pounds, I'm five feet six inches tall, and he lifted me like you would a two year-old child. He lifted me till we were eye level, and then he kissed me again with those silk lips. He then lowered me slightly, sliding my body down his, until we were pelvis to pelvis and held me there and switched his grasp of me to just under my ass on my thighs to hold me in position, and then he kissed me again. I could feel him between my thighs and I couldn't contain myself anymore, and I began to moan with excitement and leaked all over it. Still holding me, he kissed me on my neck, and I could see he was now extremely aroused. It was rock hard. I wanted it in me. I couldn't take the four-play. Just give it to me or kill me 'cause I was going to die if I didn't get this man in me. He removed his rock hard penis from between my thighs and put me to the floor, but he then picked me back up and he carried me to the bed where earlier he had pulled back the covers and laid me down. He kissed me once more and went to a drawer and pulled out a condom and carefully placed it on his firm penis. I knew it was going to hurt 'cause I hadn't been touched in going on seven months, and he wasn't anywhere near close to small. He climbed over me, and the size of his body shaded me like an eclipse of the moon in front of the sun. He laid his weight on me and I exhaled. I couldn't handle it. He could have slapped me around and I would have sent him a card. He moved in to enter me. The tip of his penis was so warm, as soon as he rubbed his second head across my clitorus I came. I was breathing so heavy I thought I was going to pass out. He was kissing me to calm me, but it only made it worse. He pushed and I popped up a little, and he moaned at the thought of how tight I was going to feel, and how wet I was. He gripped me firmly to keep me from running, and began once more. I grabbed his arm as tight as I could as he pushed into me. After a few painful but gentle pushes he was in, and we both let out a sigh of relief. It felt like I had swallowed life; he was so deep inside of me. I was quivering in his arms, and I had cum once more. He licked me all over and sucked on my nipples in such a way that his large tongue seemed to massage them. He hadn't moved since he'd been in. He just wanted us to feel each other for a moment. He was preparing to love me. He wrapped his big arms under me and supported my neck and then slowly in and out he moved. The earth began to shake and I felt like I was on fire. He worked his hips like he was kneading dough and stirring a cup of warm tea. I moaned softly but loud almost like whining. It was turning him on. We were body to body. There was no air that existed between us. He kissed me and watched me scream and unfold in his arms. He put his lips to my ear and whispered in it. "Am I hurting you?" All I could do was nod my head no. "Does it feel good?" and again, I slowly nodded. "Tell me." He said softly. I couldn't say it. I was already broken. I couldn't say it and I shook my head no. "Oh, Simone, please!" The man who had broken everything in me was begging me! "Yes." I said with tears in my eyes. "Yes, Yes." He moaned and held me a little tighter, and he pushed a little harder. He was about to explode soon because his movements increased in speed. He softly dug into me as if to plug himself into my soul, and into my heart. He moaned. "Simone" He moaned some more. "Simone" The tears kept coming and I kept saying, "Yes." He was about to explode because his movements increased in speed. He was going faster, and faster, and faster, and then his body tightened and so did mine. We hit climax at the same time. He squeezed me so tightly, and I squeezed back. His massive body began to feel heavy again, which means he was slowly starting to relax. I was trembling from the whole ordeal and my bottom lip was quivering. He kisses it, and asked in a low voice how I was. "Did

I hurt you?" "No" I said, still wiping tears from my eyes. I don't know why, but I couldn't stop crying. He kisses my forehead and asks, "Did I do something?" I put my hand over my face and replied, "No, I'm so embarrassed." He smiled at me with those pearly white teeth. "Simone, don't be." I'm not sure if he believed me or not, but I told him, "I don't usually do this sort of thing. I've never slept with someone the.." He put his fingers to my lips to hush me. He leaned and gave me the most endearing kiss, and then removed his presence from mine. He went into the bathroom to remove the condom full of his wonderful genetics. I heard some water running and not long after he came out of the bathroom, turned out the light, and then walked over to the bed with a washcloth. He wiped the sweat from my head, my neck, and my stomach. He went back into the bathroom to rinse the cloth and came back to wipe my purring pussy. He also laid a towel over the giant wet spot that would soon dry up with the memory of my body's tears, and got me a glass of water. He walked over to the dresser where in the center of the candle was a pool of hot wax that had gathered due to the prolonged exposure to the fire. He took a deep breath, pressed his lips together, and the room became dark. The only light was that which peaked in from the moon as if to look in on two lovers. It settled on his back as his body shielded my eyes from the light with his large frame. I turned to face him. He kissed me on my forehead, and then wrapped me in those arms tight like he had to guard me from all in the world. This place, in his arms, is where I stayed until morning. I fell in love with him that night. I now know how women get all dick-whipped and stuff, but this shit was ri-dick-ulous. I ain't never felt no shit like this before. When I woke up in the morning he was gone, no note, no nothing. I felt so bad. I felt used, in a good way though. I found a shirt and went to look around. His apartment was really nice. Large furniture was in the living room just like in the bedroom. The golden rays of the sunlight poured into the apartment like fresh lemonade. It awakened me from the sleepwalking bliss my body was floating in. The apartment looked like something out of a Crate and Barrel magazine. I liked it, he had taste. Although I felt like a used tissue, I don't know why I didn't just get my stuff and leave never to return, but I looked for a towel in the bathroom linen closet and I found one with a matching washcloth. Wine, the same color of the sheets in the bedroom, was the color of my washcloth and towel. I wanted to take a shower. If he wasn't going to have anything to do with me anymore, then I was going to soak all this up while I could. The shower had a deep tub suited for the large man to sit in and be cozy. I noticed there were still small drops of water on the sink and in the tub. He got dressed and left, and I didn't hear a thing. I pulled back the plaid black, bone, and wine colored thick cotton shower curtain and matching plastic shower curtain liner, and turned the knob to release the hot liquid destined to soothe me this morning. In the shower I thought about the night before and how that man touched more than just my breasts and how my body was calling out, and how he answered. My clit was so sensitive I had a hard time washing without my nipples getting hard and my toes curling. I felt like a crackhead. My body was calling him now but I knew he couldn't hear me, or did he? That shower felt so good but it didn't wash away what I still felt inside. I thought I had a pretty good judge of character and knew what people were about. Could it have been that last night I knew and didn't care? Could it have been the way he went about it? I don't know. I just want to get dressed and leave. I walked out the bathroom and the smell of his colon was fresh in my nose since I had washed him from my body. I walked out into the bedroom and I dropped my towel in front of his dresser and slid my fingers across the beautiful wood structure. I felt like Alice in wonderland 'cause it seemed too big for me but I loved it. I picked up his colon and smelled it, I couldn't help myself. I took a spray and with every drop of that mist to my skin I became more aroused. I closed my eyes and took a moment. "I'm beginning to think you like my colon more than me." He… scared… the… shit.. out of me. I'm glad he said something when he did 'cause

I think I was about to start touching on myself and he would have been like this bitch is crazy! Ha Ha. I laugh at the thought of that moment every so often. "I apologize." I said. "I just wanted to freshen up before I left." He just stood there and he had a look on his face like—okay get dressed then. I turned around and I started putting on my clothes that were in a neat pile from last night. I put on my pleated skirt with no underwear 'cause they had yesterday's juices on them, and I was just out the shower. The whole time I got dressed he didn't say anything. I bent over to tie my sneakers, totally forgetting I had no panties on. For him to be as big as he is, he can surely move fast and quietly. As I just began to tie the last sneaker his hands were on my hips and he was lifting my skirt exposing my nude bottom. He bent over me while I was still face down and whispered in my ear. "I don't want you to go." Both of us, still bent over, only now he had turned me to face the high bed and brace myself. His body was warm. I could feel it because somewhere in between the time I turned around to tie my kicks, and when he walked over to me, he had removed his crisp white t-shirt that he wore with a pair of gray baggy Timberland sweatpants, and a pair of white Air Force Ones. I could also feel through those sweatpants what the thought of a newly washed pussy was making him feel. He kissed the back of my neck and my nervous system screamed with excitement. What makes a woman feel this way with a man? I couldn't refuse him, not even on his worst day. Still resting himself on my back, he slid his hands up and down my chest firmly touching me and grabbing my breasts and squeezing my nipples. "Can you stay?" He said as he began to slide his sweatpants down while still pressed up against me. What the hell does he mean? Can I stay??!! Hell yeah I can stay! You got me bent over a bed rubbing every surface and pressing every button and I'm just going to say no?? Like I said, he knew what he did to me. He felt so good to me, like a walking dream. I swore up and down that the last twenty-four hours had been a dream. It was getting to be early evening. I had slept for a long time and I was up late last night. "Yes,

I can stay." I said in a calm before the storm voice. His deep voice, when he spoke, vibrated the hair on the back of my neck. "I've never met anyone that makes me feel the way you do." He said as he took a step back. I began to feel his face softly gliding down the center of my back. Arms still braced for impact, I waited to feel him. His face kept going, down to the small of my back, the crack of ass, all the way down. His tongue was so large and warm. I began to just melt, and had a hard time standing. He licked me in little circles and in straight lines, and sideways. He laid me at the edge of the bed, face up, and pulled me to him for more. As he placed my knees to my chest, I could hear him sucking and kissing. His moans vibrated my clit in his mouth. Last night that man made love to me, but now, today, we were gonna fuck, and hard I presume. It didn't take long for me to break and my climax was met. He then pulled me off the bed and flipped me back over with no effort at all, so that once more I could brace myself for what was to come. My knees were still weak from his tongue workout. I heard the sound of a small wrapper and not long after a firm grip on my shoulder and a stiff dick inside me. When he entered me the world got quiet. He wasn't the type to just jump in and start screwing. He liked you to feel him, all of him. He began short hard thrusts, with which each one I yelled. He moaned. "Uh!" He pulled my hair out of the ponytail it was in, and got a good hand full. This is what he held now to keep me from running. His short slow thrusts turned into fast jabs. We were both screaming now. Well, not literally. I was screaming and he was moaning really, really loudly. He pushed me onto the bed so that he was now lying on top of me from behind. Hard long thrusts are what the strokes turned into. He wrapped his arms around me in a bear hug, and deep into me he went. His body tightened, and his breathing got heavy. I thought he was going to crush me. He was squeezing me so tight when he climaxed. He then fell limp alongside me while still laying on me. Blair came so hard I thought he folded inside out. I was beat up, but in a good way. He just held me and asked, "I didn't hurt you? I'm sorry I got so rough, you excite me." I released my grip of his comforter, and controlled my breathing. "I'm fine." He removed himself from me yet again, and just lay on his back with the condom on. I just lay there as well. He got up and took the condom off and went into the bathroom and repeated the same routine from last night. He washed and brought the warm washcloth for me. On the way back to the bed he took off all his sweatpants and briefs and climbed back in the bed where I was still worn the hell out. He began to undress me 'cause I still had on everything but underwear. He turned on the flat screen fifty-two inch screen TV, put in a DVD, and got under the covers where I had placed myself after I was nude once more. "I want to be with you." He said. "I want you to be with me. I'll never mistreat you or cheat. I don't have any kids and never been married. I want a wife and some kids someday, and now that I've met you, I think someday is soon. So, will you be my lady?" I was in total shock. If I weren't lying down a bitch would have fell down, you understand. I rolled over and looked him dead in his face for some sign of ill will, but it wasn't there. He was serious as a heart attack. I thought this has to be some kind of dream, or a horrible life joke. I will never smoke no weed from those Jamaicans again. I was on some kind of drug that had me in a dream world, so I figured as long as I'm here, I'll enjoy. "Yes, I'll be your lady. I'll be whatever you need me to be." He looked at me with those deep brown eyes and said, "You know, when I walked over to you on the dance floor I was nervous." "Nervous of what," I said in shock. "That you wouldn't dance with me." He giggled a bit. I laughed so hard when he said that I could have died from suffocation. "I had seen you once before around the university but I was on my way to an appointment. I wanted to talk to you then but I couldn't, but I swore if I saw you again that I would say something to you." He continued, "At the club that night I didn't dance not one time. I smoked a little, and had a few drinks but that's it. A lot of women came up to me to dance and stuff but I turned them down. My friends were blowing my phone up this morning 'cause they wanted to know who I had left the club with." I could listen to him talk for hours. "When you were sleeping I went to the store and got something for breakfast so if you were hungry I could feed you. I was hoping and praying that I made it back before you woke up and left or something without even leaving a number for me to call. I didn't think about that till after I got to the store. I didn't call 'cause I knew you wouldn't pick up the phone. You don't know how turned on I was to find you in the shower. I stepped in the closet, --walk-in closet--, to hide from you until you came out." I was speechless... and, in love. You know how sometimes you know something dumb is going to happen but you can't stop it? What made me say it, I don't know, but it just came out quicker than a gay man at Fort Dicks. "I wish I could stay in this moment forever. I think I love you. I feel like I've loved you my whole life." I done fuckin' did it now. This man thinks I'm the hell crazy. He smiled, curled up next to me and whispered, "I love you too." And we kissed. We kissed like two people discovering kissing for the first time. That is how we spend the rest of that Sunday evening and many more evenings for two and a half years. We became like white on rice after that. My mother thought he was the cutest thing on two legs and dad loved the fact that he loved his baby girl. We moved together to Atlanta when I graduated 'cause of the job offer that I am currently working at. He operated his business from Atlanta, and when he got settled in he opened another branch of High Rise here as well. Our love making never had a dull moment. Everything was running smooth. Both of us working, and loving each other, smokin' and stuff. We had everything. His family was in Jamaica but I talked to his mother every time he did. She loved me. He had one older brother and sister, and two younger brothers. I met one brother, Marvin, that had flown in on holiday to come see him. Marvin was coming into town to make some money and I'm not talking about the legal kind either, but Blair loved his brother. Marvin was going to stay for a month, and he tried to kiss me when Blair wasn't around one day. It was just he and I in the apartment. Marvin looked just like Blair only he was much darker and his hair was short and coarse. Marvin also, was nowhere near as big as Blair was, but you could definitely see they were in the same gene pool. I was getting undressed one day after I had come in from work and Marvin stopped by. Blair made him a key so he could come in if we weren't home. Blair trusted he wouldn't bring none of that drug business into our home, and he didn't. He was staying in a motel 'cause of it, and that was his choice. He came in the bedroom, and I was in some panties and a bra when he walked in. He turned around and left, but not soon after I was done and came out. I was cool about it and stuff, you know, 'cause to me it wasn't that big of a deal. "Dude next time knock before you just start entering rooms and shit!" I said. "Yo, I'm sorry. I didn't mean to do that though." He replied. "I'm good but just knock next time." I casually snapped back. Blair called and said he wanted to go play some ball with some of his boys and that he'd be a little late. I told him his brother was there and he said he'd try not to be out too long. Later, after putting a hoagie together for Blair so he could have a snack when he came in, I went to go take a shower and get myself together for tomorrow. It was Thursday evening and I wasn't about to cook, and I know he don't feel like doing anything after he comes in from playing ball except me, so this would hold him over. If he wanted more he could get take-out. I stayed up with Marvin for a little while talking about Blair, and how he and Blair would jump off waterfalls as kids in Jamaica, and how they almost killed themselves on time just missing some sharp rocks below. Blair called and said he was on his way and I told him I'd be in bed when he got there 'cause I had a long day. My access pass wasn't working, there was a fire in the fuel development room, and it was just one of those days. "Aw baby, I'll be home real soon to tuck you in. What's Marvin doing?" "Talking to some chicken head on the phone." I replied. Marvin turned and smiled 'cause he knew I was right; some girl that want to fuck him 'cause he had money. That was his favorite. When they found out he wasn't giving them shit they would stop calling him but by then he had got what he wanted. He'd always be like," Hook me up with that Louise friend of yours! I want a smart woman with her own money!" I'd look at hime and laugh. "Yeah but don't no smart woman want anything to do with the likes of you crazy." I'd say. After I got off the phone with Blair, and I made sure to tell him I love him, I got off the phone and headed towards my bedroom. I loved his bedroom furniture so we kept it when we moved. Marvin was coming up from the bathroom and as I was passing him I went to give him a good night hug like I had done so many times before. "Alright Marv I'm going to bed." "It's still early though." He protested. "I know but I had a long day and I'm tired and sleepy, so I'm gonna climb in bed and wait for your brother to come home." Shoot, I forgot to tell Blair about his sandwich. Oh well, he can take it for lunch if he gets something on the way home. That's what was on my mind after I said I was waiting for Blair. I leaned in to give him a hug and after I hugged him he wouldn't let me go. "Come on Marvin I'm tired and I want to get some rest before your brother gets home." When I said that his eyebrow went up thinking about me having sex with his brother. While he was still bear hugging me (must run in the family) he started kissing my neck and I pushed him back. Then he tried to act like he was playing. I didn't say a word. He knew he fucked up. I turned and went into the room and he left right after 'cause he knew I was going to tell Blair and he would fuck him up. I came out my room after I heard the door to the apartment close. I found the key on the coffee table when I went to shut the lights and things off in the living room. Fifteen minutes later Blair walked in. "Hey baby!" He said before kissing me. "I'm gonna just get in the shower 'cause I know you don't like me sweaty and funky!" I smiled. I didn't mind him being sweaty, it was just the funky part I had a problem with. I loved to see him with sweat, just as I liked to see him in the shower. I've done nothing but want that man since I first saw him oh so long ago. I tell him not to tell his friends how we met, you know sleeping together the first time we laid eyes on each other. For men that shit is cool to them, not women though. He always says, "Stop worrying about it 'cause we're still together aren't we? So, you can tell them you put it on me that first night, and since I've been hooked. Which is true!" He always looks at me and smiles when he says that part. I would watch him shower whenever I could. It was something about that man and water that I couldn't tear myself away from. As soon as I heard the water I would crack the door and watch him bathe himself. Even though men and women do the same things like bathe and drink soda, drive, and so many other things, we do them differently. I would watch the way he held his washcloth and the way he'd brush his teeth. He doesn't care that I watch him this way either. He just looks at me, and smiles. I watch him some time after we make love; fall asleep with his face nestled in my breasts. As I stood in that doorway that night looking at him, as I've done so many times before, I thanked God for sending an angel to watch over and be good to me. As the steam filled the bathroom the contrast between the cool bedroom and the hot bathroom made my nipples hard. I just got out the shower not too long ago, but his body in that water just looked so inviting. His jet-black hair lay back smooth like satin. Before I knew it was removing my clothes. I slowly opened the glass door and stepped in and shut it. I pressed my entire body up against the back of his, and I reached up to rub his shoulders and his back. "Why are you so good to me?" "'Cause I love you, I'm your lady, or you desire it? Pick one!" He turned around and kissed me. He would kiss me so intimately that my knees would get weak. On time I actually fainted. He brings that shit up all the damn time too. "You're the one with the fires and things goin' on and stuff, you need the rub." He was tall so he just reached over my shoulders and rubbed my back while I wrapped my arms around him and held on for dear life. He loved to see me melt in his arms. He reached down and grabbed one leg under the knee, and I gladly gave him the other. I loved when he picked me up, and he would do it nice and slow this way. It was something about this that made him cum quick, and me too. He held me like I was nothing. With the muscles in his arms all tight, he would just place his dick at my pussy and lean back so that my own weight would drop me on it. He moaned the whole way in. A few soft in and out strokes and we were both happy. I think he was waiting for some all day. No, we didn't use a condom this time. We've been together two years. We knew each other very well, and he was good at pulling out. We wouldn't have minded kids though. We had lots of money saved between the two of us, and our jobs weren't too shabby either so we were good. We rinsed his love juice off the glass door, rinsed ourselves off, and then got out. This thing with his brother was making me feel bad, partly because I knew Blair loved and trusted his brother, he hadn't seen Marvin in a long time, and then he does something like this. After we dried and lotion, Blair got some orange ginger massage oil off the dresser that we bought from Bath and Body Works, and while he lay next to me he kissed and massaged my back. "Baby, what's wrong? I know there's something on your mind. Is it today at work, you know with the lab and stuff? Simone, they'll fix all that and your research is saved and untouched." I just looked forward. "No, it's not that baby." "Then what is it? We talk about everything!" I could tell he was about to get upset 'cause I keep nothing from him and he knows it, so the fact that he has to ask, I could tell, wasn't sitting too well with him. He knew I had something to say. "Did someone do something to you!" He jumped up. I have never seen so much hate in his face in my life. "Tell me what the fuck happened!" He scared me. "Baby stop yelling, okay. Okay." "I'm sorry baby, but.." I cut him off and told him to calm down. "The reason I didn't tell you right away was because I didn't want you to be hurt." He looked like he had seen a ghost. Blair sat at the edge of the bed and prepared himself for what I was about to say. If there was ever a time that I thought he didn't love me this definitely would have changed my mind. He calmed down. I mean the way he was looking was like I was going to tell him I was leaving him or something. Both of us still naked, 'cause that's how we sleep most nights. I sat behind him and wrapped my arms around him and pressed my lips to his back. "What are you thinking right now?" I wanted to know just what he thought was going to come out my mouth. "I don't know! So many things are running through my mind." "Blair, baby, I'm not going anywhere. No one else gets my lovin', my time, or my heart baby. I'll be yours until the day you say you don't want me to be, and even then it better be a good reason 'cause I'm not leaving that easy." I felt his body take a short breath as if he were crying, and I got up and got off the bed and lifted his face; a tear had left his eye. I had never seen him like this and in a crazy way it made me want him so bad. I started kissing him all over his face. I started crying too, I'd never seen him like this. When a man brakes like that in front of you over you, he lives, eats, and breathes you. I don't think a man crying is a sign of weakness, it's a sign of strength. It takes a real man to cry in front of his woman, especially if he's crying about her. "Oh, baby. I'm here. I'm here. I'm not going anywhere unless you're coming with me. Okay, oh my God baby please know this, but what I'm going to tell you, you're not going to like it." I took a deep breath and he just sat with this blank look on his face like he could kill someone, waiting to see what I was going to say 'cause he knew now that it had to do with me. "Your brother.." Before I could finish my sentence I saw hell in his face. He jumped up and started putting on some clothes and then stopped, and came over back to where I was sitting on the floor in front of the high bed, and knelt down on one knee, picked me up and put me on the bed. "Finish telling me." "What are you going to do?" "Simone!" He yelled aggravatedly. "Okay, Okay. I went to give him a hug goodnight, like I do with all our friends and family, and when he was holding me he started licking my neck and I pushed him off me. He tried to act like he was playing but he knew he fucked up baby, he knew. He left right after it happened. I went back out into the living room after he left and his key was on the table." I thought he was going to explode. "Simone when did this happen?"

"Not long after I got off the phone with you." He started to finish getting dressed. I knew there was nothing I could say to stop him or nothing I could do. He called Marvin's cell phone and he didn't answer. So, Blair left him a message. "So, you know what happens in Jamaica when you put your hands on things that don't belong to you. You might have forgotten, but I'm going to remind you." And he hung up. Blair went into the closet. He was dressed in some black jeans, a black hoody, and black Timberland boots. I heard a click, and that could only be the sound of something I knew all too well; one of our matching nickel-plated desert eagle pistols, and a loaded chamber and clip. I jumped up. "Blair don't be stupid! Blair! Blair!" I screamed. I jumped on him and wrapped my legs around his waist and my arms around his neck. I was crying and screaming. "Blair please! I'm not going to lose you to a jail! You can't leave me! He's not worth it!" I kept screaming. He was walking around the room with me latched to the front of him 'cause my size is nothing compared to his. He tried to get me off of him and he was strong but it was going to take the power of God to make me let go with my consent. "Please! Please! Blair, Please! I love you! I can't live without you." Nothing I said seemed to be getting through to him. I was scared for real. Trying to pull me off had worn him out a little, especially since he was already a bit beat from playing ball, and sexing with me in the shower. He just sat down on the large deep cushion couch from a little mom and pop Italian furniture shop. The things we kept in the house were bought for holding his big structure, which had engulfed him when he rested his frame with me on it. I was still crying even now. "Blair, please don't do it." I was whispering in his ear. "Please. I don't know what I'd do without you in my life. I love you so much. You make me lose all control. I'm losing all control." I began to loosen my grip on him. "If you kill him you have to kill me too 'cause that's what you're doing to yourself and to me when they take you away." "He can't get away with this baby." He said in the coldest voice I've ever come out of an angry man. "Not this way baby, not this way."

I kissed him on the side of his face. He wasn't even touching me. He was just sitting there with the gun in his right hand resting on his right knee, and his left hand in a glove resting on his left knee. I felt like my world was over. I had never felt like this before, not even with my first so-called love. This was different. The very thought of that man made hell seem like a vacation as long as he was there with me. I can't remember life before him but I can damn sure see what's to come as long as he's around. I whispered and kissed some more. This mutha fucker was so damn mad I though he was going to kill himself. "Baby it's okay. I'm all yours and yours alone. You're the only one that makes me feel the way you do. No one turns me on the way you do." He put the gun on the table beside the chair. He rested his chin on my shaking shoulder. He realized what he was doing to me and just shook his head. He took off his gloves and wrapped his arms around me. "I'm sorry babe." He said in a calm exhausted voice. "I'm sorry." He stood up but this time he was carrying me instead of me holding on. He took me to the bedroom and lay with me on the bed. He wanted to part with me and I jolted to hold on. "I'm just going to take off my clothes baby. I'm coming to bed." He turned off the lights and shut the apartment down, and locked the door. Before doing those things though, he took all his clothes off. Everything was pitch black 'cause now we had thick black out velvet drapes that didn't let in a stitch of light. The only light that shined was the little night light in the bathroom from under the door. I slept on my back, which made me an easy target when he wanted to have me. For some reason it was dead quiet in the room. He walked over to the bed and he stopped in front of me. I opened my eyes, though I couldn't see too much, I saw his outline facing me. He crawled up onto the large bed and over me. He laid himself on top of me and I wrapped my arms around his neck as he rubbed me tenderly. For the first time since we'd been together I was hoping he didn't want sex. I was so out of it from what happened that I just wasn't in the mind frame for it. I guess I was sort of mad at him 'cause he let something so petty come so close to taking him from me. I was just mad. How could he even consider doing something like that? He was a big man but guns don't care how big you are. Marvin would have tried to defend himself and then it would have been all types of bullets flying everywhere. The thought of losing him made me sick to my stomach. I loved Blair, but part of me didn't want to feel this way 'cause of how bad I'd feel if he were to leave me or be taken from me. I would have stood by his side while he was in jail, but he doesn't know what that would do to me. While these thoughts are running through my mind I noticed his head has slid down past my belly button and still, slowly, climbing downward. He slid the cover off me so he was no longer kissing the Tommy Hifigure sheets, but now reacting skin. He rubbed his mustache that he recently decided to grow into the low bush between my legs. He was sorry and was about to show me. My mind may not have wanted it but my body said, "Fuck you bitch!" When his tongue reached the part of my pussy that split, he stuck his long thick tongue straight down in to taste his meal. It was then that the stiffness I was trying to maintain melted away like ice when hot water runs over it. I, once more, was bent to his will. Like I said before, I couldn't resist him. His every wish from now until the day I die would be my command. He spread my legs, and I opened up wide per unsaid instructions, and let him lick me. He reached up and firmly grabbed my breast as he let the weight of his head drive me crazy. This felt different than all the other times. I couldn't explain why I felt the need to run, or why I felt I could fly, or why I was falling even more in love than I was. Just when I thought I couldn't reach a new high, this man would grab my hand and take me there. I whined my hips slowly into his thick silk lips, and danced with his tongue held firmly between the lips of my mouth; and not the ones on my face. I'm losing all control. I lost all control. His tongue massages me to my climax and I feel it in the pit of my stomach, so…., I vomited off the side of the bed. He loved when I ran from him when we were committing any sexual act. It brought him great pleasure to break me in that way, which is what he thought was happening when I clawed my way over to the edge. When he heard the noise of the thick liquid hitting the floor he jumped up, and turned on the light. "Are you okay baby!" He was rubbing my back. I was just laying over the side of the bed breathing, trying to bring my heart rate back to normal. He started smiling at me like he was on drugs. He ran into the bathroom to get a wet cloth to wipe my mouth. When he came back he was still smiling. I had to ask. "What the hell are you smiling at me like that for?" He stopped and said, "Are you pregnant?" He was actually excited about the thought of the whole thing. "No, I'm not." "Oh." The thought of it crossed his mind and lit him up. That changed his whole mood from sad to real happy real quick. I might as well have been pregnant 'cause that's how he began to treat me. I went to get up and get a toothbrush and shit to brush my teeth, and some mouthwash to rinse. He brought me my toothbrush and toothpaste with a small cup of Listerine. I started brushing my teeth while he wiped up the puke off the floor. The whole time we've been together I haven't thrown up. That's love, cleaning up someone else's throw-up; he seemed to do it with a smile. This shit was too much for me. I thought I was going to lose my mind from all these changes I'd been put through in the last few hours. It was one o'clock in the morning and I had to get up for work in a few hours at six o'clock, and I felt like shit. After I was done brushing my teeth he brought the bathroom trash can so I could spit in it. He wiped my mouth and the whole time I just looked at him. After all the mess was cleaned up, mess meaning me, he got back in bed with the lights still turned on. He sat straight up and looked straight ahead. I looked at him and turned on my side away from him facing the window on the right side of the bed, if you were looking at dead on. He just sat there while I felt like, "what the hell else could I don't in front of this man to make me look stupid?" He got up, turned off the light and curled up to me. He put his mouth over my ears. "Baby can I tell you something?" I didn't answer but he continued, "See, sometimes people do stupid things, and sometimes we can't control ourselves, and we do things we know are wrong. Baby I'm only human and I just can't bear the thought of another man having you other than me." He was holding me tight while saying this, as if to let me know I was his only focus. "Baby there will be no other. As long as you are good to me, I'll be here for you always." I rolled over and embraced him, and then we slept the sleep of the dead. After only having a few hours of sleep I rolled out of bed. I was so tired and it was so dark in the room that I hadn't noticed Blair wasn't in the bed until I got out the shower and turned on the light. I ran into the living room and he wasn't there either. I called his cell phone, which was ringing inside the ball shorts he was wearing the night before. I felt sick. I had to get dressed and go to work. I got dressed and I had a cup of coffee. I don't usually drink it but for some reason I needed it today. I usually drink coffee at night after dinner to cap off a meal but I wasn't a morning coffee head. I waited hoping the phone was going to ring, but it didn't. It was time for me to go 'cause if I stayed any longer I was going to be late for work, and I had a fire to deal with. I gathered my briefcase, and checked my black Armani suit and Liz Claiborne heels in the mirror. I also made sure my little longer than shoulder length hair, though it was out, was in place and flowing. I took a deep breath and went to walk out the door. I opened the door and there he was all sweaty. He came in and kissed me. "Hey babe!" He said casually. "Hey babe? Hey babe? Where the hell were you at?" "I just went for an early morning run to clear my mind. I had a lot running through my mind, and needed air." It wasn't odd for him to run like that because I got him doing it. I worked out and went to the gym every chance I could and so did he. I started him running 'cause I told him it was good for his heart, and we're not getting any younger. I was twenty-five when I met him and he was twenty-eight. Two years later, well one year eleven months, we were still rockin' and rollin'. "I couldn't sleep and I didn't want to wake you by moving all over the apartment, so I went for a run." I just looked at him and walked out the door. I was getting in my car and he came running across the street with no shirt on and his curls bouncing. I rolled down my window and before I could say anything out my mouth, he had his tongue in it. "I love you." "I love you too." Work was crazy. I showed up to the lab and before I could even get my coat on they were in my face, needing files, access codes. We assessed the situation and calculated money, time, and research lost; I mean it was a crazy day. I was on the phone making orders for petroleum, C4, phosphorus, and other explosive materials that you have to give DNA up to be able to access. I was glad for all the confusion though 'cause it kept my mind from wondering where Blair had been while I was sleeping. By the time I got everything as caught up as I could get things until our lab was rebuilt, I looked up at the clock and it was six forty five at night. Damn. I had been here a whole lot longer than I wanted to be, and it was time to roll out. After talking with a few of my senior lab partners, we decided that we had to shut our current project down for a few weeks until they could get the lab up and running at full speed again. So, basically I was going on paid vacation, something I could really use! I went to my desk and packed up a few notebooks and charts, so that I could work on some reports and things on my fully loaded Dell desktop computer, set inside of a mahogany secretary with a pull out keyboard and six in one printer. I loved that computer. It was expensive but I used that computer for everything it was worth. On the car ride home I was in a daze. The sky seemed to never move and I was in a movie that didn't have an ending; time was nothing in my mind. I got in the house at about seven thirty to find him sleeping on the couch with the TV on. I didn't want to wake him, so I softly walked past him and dropped the paperwork by the computer and headed for the shower. I turned on some Nina Simone and let the hot water and her voice take me to a place not easily reached by car, plane, or my imagination. Nina really knew how to do it. By the time I got out the shower there was a plate of cheese and fruit with a tall frosted flute of champagne on a tray in the middle of the room, with some red and pink roses on it. The door to the room was closed 'cause he knew when Nina came on that there were some things going on and I need quiet. He was trying to say sorry, but for what? I drank my champagne and ate my cheese and crackers while Nina sang. All hush now, while Nina sang. I came out the room and he was sitting in front of the TV as if to be waiting for me. I sat next to him and he kissed me and asked me how my day was. He was so jumpy; ready to jump at my every move. He bent over whenever I said something but this time was different. I just looked at him. I love this man so much; I kissed him and laid my head on his shoulder. I picked up the remote and turned to the nine o'clock news. I watched for a moment at all the fucked up things that are going on in this world. I told him how I was on a paid vacation for a while 'cause they had to rebuild the lab and he was too happy. He went to work but he didn't have to 'cause he owned the business and he had enough workers to do the job for him. He only went to give him something to do 'cause I was going to work and I wasn't home. Besides, he had a thing about his woman getting up and going to work while he slept. He thought that kind of thing was corny. Next thing I know, some well-dressed newswoman, whose make-up looked like it was painted on, read her commentary. "A man was found shot dead in his car in the Crown Royal hotel's underground parking lot at nine o'clock this morning. Marvin Cacilus was found shot three times in the chest while sitting in his car." I jumped up and ran toward the bathroom and threw up again. He came in there after me. He didn't have to say anything and I wasn't going to either. I just looked at him. I've tossed my cookies twice in less than a twenty-four hour time frame. I need a damn vacation. I knew now what my man was capable of when it came to what he loved and held dear. I knew now that he would protect me no matter what the cost. He loved me, loved me enough to kill his own brother for touching me. You know, I think he killed him because he was his brother. If it would have been some strange man he would have just beat him down like he did one time we were in Philadelphia at Penn's Landing. A man tried to talk to me and I told him I was with someone and he wouldn't take no for an answer. Blair came over 'cause he heard the fuss and told the dude I was with him, and we walked off. The guy walked up and grabbed my arm away from Blair's, and the next thing I know I saw Blair's shiny platinum pendant whirl around, and the sun blocked by his massive arm swinging over my head, and then I turned to see the man out cold on the ground. Blair quickly grabbed me and we left. He was pissed after that shit so we just left. We went back to the apartment 'cause his day was just ruined, and I couldn't have a good time if he was upset. We were going to eat at Dave and Buster's, which is a little further up Delaware Ave on the waterfront, but the sunny summer day was done. There was only one thing that can calm a man down after fighting for his woman, which is his woman. I knew he was mad so I kind of left him alone to watch his sports and stuff, and cool down. I took a shower to wash off some of the faint summer sweat. I dried off, lotion, put on his favorite oil and walked into the living room butt naked. I sat next to him and a part of every woman feels it's a little of her fault, but not in a bad way. We can't help it if we look good. One wish all men share is to have a woman that is good looking, smart, wifey material, and a hoe in the bedroom, but they don't want anyone else to want her either. They want her to be seen but not noticed, like a painting in an art gallery. Look but don't touch. He tried not to look at me but I knew my freshly washed body was, and always would be, a turn on to him no matter how he tried to fight it. He liked to wear sweatpants in the house; they were comfy to him, and it made his manhood easy to touch through the cotton material. I rubbed him as he watched the TV, trying to ignore me but other body parts were saying different. I reached in and pulled his third arm out, exposing it to the room temperature and eased it into my mouth. He inhaled a deep breath and cleared his throat. I got off the couch and got on my knees in front of him and pulled him to me. I sucked his dick like it was the only way to save my life. He was grabbing everything around him. He was still trying to play hardball though! Okay. Just when he was about to let go of his load, I stopped. I stopped as suddenly as I started, walked into the bedroom, and shut the door. I know he must have been sitting there going crazy 'cause a few minutes after he came in the room, dick still out, to find me pleasuring myself since he wanted to act stupid. I was rubbing my titties and rubbing my pussy and making some soft noises. He took off his t-shirt and pulled down his sweats to just above his knees, 'cause he knows I like when he makes love to me in sweats, and came to the bed. When he tried to pull me close, I pushed him away. When he tried to climb on top, I pushed him away. I started moaning louder and his dick started to drip. I knew he was hurting. Still, he tried to touch me and I refused. He couldn't take it anymore. He grabbed me by the ankles, pulled me to him, and I fought the whole way. He picked me up and wrapped my legs around his waist and stuck it in. I let him have three good strokes before I pushed myself off and back on the bed. He was mad now. He grabbed my hands with his large hands and held them up over my head. He used his massive legs to spread mine, and with his free hand held me in place. He rammed me, and I tried to kick and get away but he wasn't playing with me anymore, and he rammed me some more. I was screaming from all the pain, good pain though, and trying almost my hardest to get away from him. One of my hands got free and I gave him a good scratch across the chest and he let out a deep grunt of pain. He grabbed my hands now, one in each of his and fucked my IQ higher. We were both screaming and when he came, his load was hot and thick. I could feel it and I wrapped my legs around him 'cause I didn't want him to pull out. He tried but I wouldn't let him so he gave in and filled me up. We couldn't pipe like that too often 'cause the doctor said I wouldn't have any walls left. For one month we couldn't have sex so I could retain my density and he was not happy with that, but we did plenty of other things that put us to sleep. With my legs around his waist and his knees in the kneeling position, he rested half of his frame on me. He was sweating something fierce. I was kissing his forehead while he was catching his breath. "I love you." He said. "I know!" He was cut bad. There were four claw marks on his left breast muscle and when he finally sat up, I could see that I had drawn a little more blood than intended. He had bled on me as well. After I snapped my backbone back into place I got up and cleaned his sex wound. He was going to have that scar forever. I never asked him about Marvin and he never talked about it. I acted like I never knew him. Blair's mother called one day though and while I was talking to her about different things she asked about Marvin. I didn't know what to say. "Well Miss D, he was here but he left and we haven't heard from him since." I felt like shit for lying to his mother. I told Blair about it. "What did you tell her?" He said in a serious calm voice. "I told her he was here and we haven't heard from him since he left." "Good." We soon after took a plane to the Pocono's and enjoyed two weeks of warm fireplaces and that northern woodland air we were so used to. It was here that he asked me to marry him. We were making love in front of the fireplace in our most modern log cabin after getting out of the hot tub. For some reason to me he felt different. He felt a little softer, a little gentler than before. He seemed to glow like the North star on a clear winter night, like the fire that danced on our bodies as we made love so many times before. Something about this time felt different. It felt like the first time he made me his almost two years ago. The way he touched me, the way he looked at me, the way he kissed me. Oooohh was he kissing me. His kisses alone would make me climax with him in me. As we reached our peaks we held on as if we were to be sucked away from each other and taken to a place past death. He didn't bother to pull out this time either and I didn't care. I would give this man a child every year should he so ask it. He lifted his head and looked at me with those brown eyes, and I knew something was up. He seemed sad. "Blair?" I said, rubbing his face. I could see tears welding up in his eyes. "Blair? Baby what's wrong? Tell me now."

He parted his lips to speak and everything seemed to hush for this man's words. "Simone, I don't know if the way you act is just a show or if I really have the effect on you that you say I do," I was stunned, "but, I know you really make me feel like a man. You make me feel like more of a man being with you than my dick does." And the tears kept coming. "It's true Simone. Nothing has ever made me prouder to be a man than you." I didn't know what to think. Tears started rolling down my eyes. At first I thought all that shit with his brother had caught up to him, and he was breaking. It started to scare me a little bit. He continued. The tears were coming harder and I was crying because I didn't know what was wrong. "Simone I hope that as long as I'm in your life I can make you as happy as you've made me." He reached under the pillow and pulled out a box. "Nothing would make me happier than spending the rest of my life with you. I know now there is no one else for me. Will you marry me?" As soon as I got my breath I said, "Yes, yes, yes." Both of us were crying except I was ballin'. We spent the rest of the night making love like it was our last days on earth. We were so happy. Nothing could have taken me down from the high I was on. Weezy, who I had met not long after we moved in, was so happy and she was to be my maid of honor and everything. I told my mother and father and they were happy, 'cause my mother wanted some grandkids with good hair. His mother was thrilled too. She told me she thought he'd never get married. We were very happy and I was so ready to become Mrs. Blair Armstrong, but fate as it seems had some other plans for me. Two and a half years of happy living and loving and then one day it's brought to an abrupt stop. I was at work when it happened. Got off of work a little late that night due to some late night presentations the whole staff was working on for a new product for soldiers to use in the field. A new form of incendiary device, about the size of a peanut, about the weight of one, and packs enough punch to level a twenty story building. It was nine forty at night and I stopped by my favorite pizza place to get some dinner and a movie from Blockbuster 'cause it was a

LITTLESHIRLY

Friday night and I had been calling the house and Blair's phone since I had left work, and he wasn't answering. I thought he was out on the courts, which he loved to do on the weekends we didn't have anything planned. I got to the apartment and called his cell phone more and still no answer. I dropped all the gear and headed straight for my old friend, the shower. When I came out I had noticed there was a message on the machine. "That's probably him now." I said to myself. I lotioned and scented myself and got dressed in some house clothes, a pair of sweatpants (go figure), and a wife beater. I got a piece of pizza and headed for the answering machine, but before I could push the button there was a knock on the door. I answered the door and there was a pale white guy at the door in a sears sucker suit flashing a badge in my face. "Miss McKnight?" I nodded my head yes while giving a look of question as to why this man was on my doorstep at this hour. "I need you to get dressed and come with me. It's about Mr. Armstrong." All time had frozen dead in its tracks. When I finally came to, I felt a burning sensation on my foot from where the hot pizza had fallen. I felt sick. "What's wrong? What happen?" I said as tears welled up in my eyes. I then noticed his partner down the hall a way back in a shadow, because the sears sucker cop turned to look at him and just told me to come with him. With every step I took through the apartment I felt more and more ill. I don't know what to think but I know in the movies when the cops come to your house it's either to take someone away or someone is dead, and they weren't asking to question me. We arrived at the hospital. The emergency room was unusually quiet and the hallways seemed longer than life. As we rounded the corner I noticed a sign that said morgue, and it had an arrow pointing in the direction we were heading in. I could tell that I must have looked awful because the sears sucker's partner was now holding me and walking me down the hall. It smelled like death and I felt like the dead. The sears sucker cop's name was Willis and Snider was the incog-negro cop in the corner. He was black. He smelled like a soft musk, like the oils the

Muslims wear. The hallway finally stopped and the big doors swung open. I walked in and it smelled like human preserves, I threw-up right there on the spot. After I got myself together they walked me over to a table, which clearly had a body on it under a sheet. I knew it was him, I knew it was Blair. There was a faint scent of his colon in the air the closer I got to the table. I started to lose it. I cried and cried, and silently the tears began to fall. I felt hollow, like someone took out my guts. The sucker cop spoke. "Miss McKnight I know this must be hard for you but we need you to identify the body." I mustered some kind of strength to nod my head yes. I pulled back the cover and there he was. He was so pale, so dead. My legs gave out and I fell to the floor. I cried so hard I thought I was going to fold inside out. He was dead. My whole world lay on that table motionless. I cried and cried some more. "Miss McKnight, he was killed in a car wreck on the expressway." I had heard about that on my way home from work. A car on the back of a tow truck was not properly secured and it broke loose on the expressway right onto Blair's car. It was a seven-car pile up, and Blair's car was in the middle of it all. I stood up and pulled the rest of the sheet back and was horrified. I screamed in horror! He was in pieces. His arm was severed from his body along with one of his legs. His whole chest was smashed in and one of his hands was missing. He was folded up in the vehicle and they had to use the Jaws of Life to get him out. "He died quickly. The blow to his head put him out first thing so he didn't suffer." Snider said, trying to reduce the screeching coming from my mouth. Willis quickly tried to cover Blair up. I kept screaming. I screamed until I passed out. I woke up in a hospital room. I looked around the room. Was it all a bad dream? I had slept really hard for some reason or another. I looked over to the chair that was on the side of the bed and found Weezy asleep in it. I moved my legs and stretched. Weezy heard my movements and quickly rushed to my bedside. "Weezy, where am I?" "You're in the emergency room. Don't panic, you're okay. You were hit pretty hard with the news and they sedated you." I couldn't remember what news she was talking about until I saw the tear starting to form in her eyes. "Weezy, tell me it's not true. Tell me it's not true. Where is Blair!?" I called out to him expecting him to come around the corner and hold me and kiss me and tell me everything was all right, but he never came. He never said it, and it was then that I knew he never would ever again. The nurses came running in with a needle full of some liquid that I'm sure was to put me down, only to find me in the arms of my best friend in the world morning my lost love. They pulled the curtain back and let me cry. I'm good friends with the president of the hospital. She was directly involved with some of the drug testing we got into from time to time as a side project with my company, and she was very "hands on." Her name was Shelby Marone. She had never been married, didn't have any kids, so she ran that hospital to a "t" because it was her life. When she had heard what happened to Blair, she had some flowers sent to my room with a card telling me to stay as long as needed. I had done a few favors for her once and she always said when the time came she was going to take care of me, and little did I know I'd be really taking her up on her offer. Weezy helped me get dressed and took me home. Weezy was just as hurt as I was 'cause she always said Blair was like the brother she never had. One time Blair smacked this guy she was going out with because he was acting out one night we had all gone out. He was all over Weezy and she was telling him to back up. Well, Blair got up, reached across the table and smacked the guy straight across his face and said, "I believe the lady said stop." The man, I think John was his name, just sat there in shock. I tried not to laugh but Weezy started it. She even looked at him and was like, "Damn!" John was so embarrassed that he just got up and left with a tear in his eye. He knew Blair would have fucked him up had he even looked like he wanted to do something. His face was red as shit and an old lady, when we left, gave Blair a high five. We laughed about that shit for days. Weezy drove me home. When we got there she put me in the jocose tub that was now next to the shower.

We had a wall knocked out and installed it two months ago. Weezy got in it all the time. Sometimes we had to kick her out. She ran me a nice hot bath and saw to it I was in. "I'll be right back Simone. I'm just gonna get some things from my apartment." By the time Weezy came back an hour later, I was dressed in some bedclothes and in bed. She came back with a big giant bag full of clothes. She only lived upstairs but I guess she didn't want to let me out of her sight. Louise was good friend to me. She called the job and told them what happened, and she would talk to my mother to let her know we were home from the hospital. The doctors called my mother, and my mother called Weezy. I had to make one phone call though. I had to call Blair's mother. I couldn't even get the words out; I was crying so badly. "Mrs. Armstrong, Blair, he's, he's. Blair he's." I just kept crying. "What's wrong with my baby?" she said now as afraid as I was when the cops came to me. "Blair, he's dead. He was killed in a car crash." She started screaming and I couldn't take it. The wale of a mother's loss was too much to bear. I had to hang up. Weezy made all the funeral arrangements and stuff. I gave her the information and showed her where all the family numbers were, and gave her the checkbook, and she took care of the rest. I just didn't have the strength. The funeral was five days later and everybody was there. I just cried. I just fell to my knees when I saw him. My mother walked me to his coffin. "Mama who it this?" I asked as if I didn't know. "That is not the beautiful man I love mama, it's not him, it's not him!" I flew his family in from Jamaica. The sisters, brothers, aunts, and uncles stayed in a hotel while both the mothers stayed with me. They told Weezy to go home 'cause they knew she needed a break to chill out, but she still came back every morning and left late at night. The only thing was she wasn't sleeping there anymore, well that is till they left. Blair took out life insurance as soon as he started in the construction business and kept it up the whole time. The lawyer came to my house and basically told me I wouldn't have to worry about money for a while, as if I did anyway. Blair's insurance was valued at four hundred fifty thousand dollars. That's almost half a million dollars. Was he putting that away and taking care of my wants and needs? Even in death that man was going to take care of me. He left me the company along with all his worldly possessions. I didn't even know he had a will made up! I just sat and cried and good old Weezy was always there for a shoulder. After everything was all said and done, I didn't go to work for a month after that. I knew I had to do something because I knew he wouldn't have wanted me to go on the way I was. I wasn't eating, I slept all day, and I wouldn't bathe for two, three days at a time. Weezy would have to come wash me. She thought I was going to die and I thought I was already dead. One night while I was sleep in bed, I had just had a bath and Weezy had shut everything down. I was good and tired but I wasn't quite asleep. It scared the shit out of me really. I was on my way to sleep and I could smell something that was more familiar to me than the smell of my own pussy, Blair's colon. It suddenly filled the room as if it had been sprayed all over. Next thing I knew I felt someone wrap their arms around me as they got in the bed. It was a man. This man was Blair. "You don't have to be afraid. I won't hurt you. I could never hurt you." The tears just came streaming out my eyes and a hurt grabbed my soul and pulled it under. I didn't turn around to see if it was him, because I knew it was. No one was in here, Weezy always locked the door, and I knew the way he held me. "I miss you so much and I love you. I'm nothing without you. Please come home or I'll just die without you." I just wanted to die to just touch him one last time. He kissed my neck and it warmed all those now cold places in my heart. That kiss took away the suffering but the pain remained. I was pitch black in the room. Not even the bathroom night light was on. I rolled over to this figure in the dark and put my face to his large baby fine chest and kissed as I had done so many times before. If this was a dream he sure felt real. "You know I never wanted to leave you, but there is nothing we can do about it now. Just know that I'll be here when it's your turn, but that's not for quite some time." "Why did he take you from me? My only joy, why?" "Simone, some things we'll all know when the time is right." He kissed my forehead and with each kiss one more tear seemed to dry away. I had also come to notice he was naked. Whatever was happening to me I liked it. If I was going crazy I didn't want to be sane. If I was living in a dream, I never wanted to wake up, and in the blink of an eye we were back on that fur rug in front of the fireplace naked in the Pocono's where he had asked me to marry him. I could see him clear as day as he was smiling at me. I reached up and hugged him. He kissed me deep and passionately like he had done so many, many times before. I melted in his arms and once again with those massive legs he spread mine and entered me. It was all so real. We made love once more in front of that fireplace where our lives had just begun. With every stroke I cried but I cried away anger, pain and frustration, but I was still mad. I was still angry so I rolled him over and climbed on top, which I didn't do too often unless I had a death wish. I dug my fingers into his massive breast muscles and I rode him. I rode him hard. It was hurting but I didn't care. I wanted to die just so I could stay with him. You know they say if you die in your dreams you don't wake up, well I was hoping he'd stab my coochie till I bled to death from it and never saw the light of day again! All that ended up happening though was I came with tender grace while my whole body cried from satisfaction. I lay once more face in his chest still on top of him telling him not to go. He told me this would be the last time I would see him and that he had to come see me because he didn't think I was going to make it. He told me it wasn't my time no matter how much I wanted it to be. I fell asleep in his chest on that rug with his arms around me. When I woke up the next morning I was naked and satisfied in my bed. The covers were all over the place and it was late into the afternoon. The other side of the bed was warm like someone had been sleeping in it all night. I no longer felt afraid to go on. I vowed that this day would be the last day I spend in bed. I enjoyed his afterglow for the last time. I spent the rest of the afternoon in bed though watching cartoons, that's what we used to do after we made love on our off days during the week. Weezy arrived after work with dinner like clockwork at eight fifteen every night, but when she came in this night I was washed and dressed, and dinner was made. I had also been talking to the gentleman who I was now about to employ to take over the company, with me still being top dog of course. I wasn't going to sell that business. Blair worked hard to get his High Rise where it was on the map and I was going to make sure I stayed there. The man's name was Lance King. I met Lance at a black successor's conference and he told me how his son had just got out of school for business management and how he aspired to run his own construction company. Blair took his card and told him if something opened up he would give him a call. Well, this was going to be his big break and I had faith in him. Time went on and with the help of a good friend, music, pizza, a little weed, and some tears. I got Blair's name tattooed on my calf, something he always wanted me to do but I wouldn't. With that tattoo I let him go and the pain from that tattoo was nothing compared to the way I miss him. As I said before Weezy was good with that money management stuff, and between her investing our money, my job, and High Rise I was set. I wanted to buy a house but there was no reason to right now. Almost two years had gone by since Blair's death and I hadn't really done much of anything that whole time. I hadn't talked to any men or gone to any clubs. Sometimes Weezy and I would go get a drink from time to time but that was after work or something. We went out and celebrated the rise in our stock one night. I had taken one hundred thousand dollars and gave it to Weezy to play with and do her thing. Next thing I know she was calling saying we were rich. She added twenty thousand to my hundred thousand and turned it into eight hundred seventy two thousand three hundred forty three dollars and eight cents. She showed up at my apartment with a bottle of Moet 'cause contrary to what people say, everyone doesn't like Crystal. She had two empty glasses and a smile bright enough to light

New York. After she got there though she thought it was too big of a deal to stay in that night, so I went out with her. We went to this little jazz place called Hush. We toasted and drank late into the night to the mellow sounds of Billie Holiday, Nina Simone, and Cassandra Wilson. It was there she handed me the check of our winnings and I immediately took out my checkbook and wrote a check for half the entire winnings. "Girl what's this?" "It's your half." She looked at me like I had skipped a math class or two. "Simone, I didn't put in enough money to get half girl." "Weezy you put in more than you think. You were the only someone there for me when I was on the wire. You saw me through some tough times. The only reason my mother left me with you is because she trusted you to be good to me and you were. I've been thinking about a way to thank you for a while and I think this is the way for me to do it." She laughed and said I was crazy. "Louise Hathaway here is your check for four hundred thirty six thousand one hundred seventy one dollars and fifty four cents. Please. Take it." Weezy now knew I was serious 'cause I wasn't laughing and tears were on their way down. "Take it! I don't want for anything, and it's the least I can do for you saving my life. I can try to make yours a little more easier, as if it were hard, but you know what I'm saying. Take it. Please!" Weezy started crying and we hugged for a little while, drank one more bottle, and headed home. My next birthday was coming up and almost two years had gone by since Blair's death and I needed to get away. I had a whole lot of vacation time saved up and I was about to lose my mind. Weezy was due for a trip as well. I had finished this big fuel project I was working on for a while, and I had time to kill for testing. We couldn't figure out where we wanted to go though. She wanted to go to Jamaica. That was out of the damn question. I would have to go see Blair's mother. I couldn't go over there and not go visit. The shit wasn't happening. I had a hard time calling his mother, let alone going to see her. "What about New Orleans?" Weezy said cheerfully for fear that I might start crying again. "Now that seems like a good idea!" Before you knew it we were making plans to head to New Orleans, Louisiana. I was thinking about starting school next year to get my master's degree in Biochemistry so it would be a good idea to take some time off before I burn my brain out. I just need to get away, you know? With Blair being gone for so long and not dating, I just wanted to run away. I've always wanted to go to New Orleans. Something about the air down there was calling me. Weezy and I, not long after, booked our flight and hotel reservations and three weeks later we were on our way. It was a good time for me and I wishBlair could have been there. Weezy being my best friend and not having to want for anything, and being financially secure, things were just good. I was lonely though. Weezy had gotten us a two-bedroom suite with a living room and a wonderful view. It was called The Grand and grand it was. The lobby of the twenty seven-story building was like something out of a movie. Even though it was daytime outside when we got to the hotel, it was bright as hell in there. It was like the sun never set in that place. The staff seemed like they never stopped smiling. We approached the front desk to check in and was met by the finest young man I had seen in a long time. "Good afternoon, and welcome to the Grand! My name is Phillip. What can I do for you two lovely ladies?" We told Phillip he could check us in and he sent for the bellman to take our things upstairs. There were many echoes of soft French and Creole spoken words in the air and just for a second I felt like I was in a foreign country until the bellman said, "This way please." The carpet was so thick it felt like I was sinking into it down to my knees. It was a deep winter green with thick threads. I had been in beds that weren't this soft. Weezy was so happy with the choice of hotel that was selected for us. She told the travel agent she wanted something, "elegantly beautiful," as she put it, but she never thought this was what she was getting. Weezy has stayed in some nice places and so have Blair and I, but this was nice. I told her you get treated a little better when you're just a few hundred dollars from being a millionaire. We arrived on the twenty fifth floor and that same thick carpet greeted us as we walked off the elevator. I know those bellmen must be strong as shit pushing those carts over this thick forest floor. The hallways were long and quiet. The walls were padded and clothed with heavy embroidered material that looked old century. It was a thick rich red color with gold lace weaved into the fabric. Weezy and I both were looking with our mouths open. We arrived at our twin suite, twenty five fifty nine. We had a room with two separate rooms with-in it. You know, for when Weezy felt like being a pimp and wanted some privacy. The room looked like something out of a LifeStyles Of The Rich and Famous magazine. The bellman forced the cart across the carpet into the room past our stunned frames and opened the curtains. The light poured in like golden hope in a world of dark confusion and I exhaled like I'd been saved. The living room was immaculate. I didn't want to touch anything for fear that its perfect fragileness would be broken. There was a fifty two inch flat tv suspended by a clear frame. I almost thought it was floating. We had a small kitchen that was all stainless steel, as if I came on vacation to cook, but anyway it was nice. I took the "A" room and Weezy took "B" simply because those were the doors we were standing next to. I had kind of lost myself in the view for a moment until I heard Weezy yell out, "There are hot tubs in the rooms!" I walked away from the breathtaking view to see what my friend was screaming about and I tripped over my purse and hit the damn floor. The carpet was so thick and soft I could have swore I bounced. I felt like Snuggle from the fabric softener commercials. I'm so glad Weezy ain't see that shit 'cause she would have laughed her ass off. I got up right before she came out of the hallway leading to her room.

"Girl, go look in your room. They put two big bottles of Cabernet Sauvignon white in mine. What did you get?"

Weezy's travel agent knows she prefers white wines to reds and so they put two big bottles in each room. I walked in the room and saw the two bottles of wine. One was placed in a bucket of ice while the other was on stand-by. The bucket was not alone. It was surrounded by a large fruit tray and a large cheese tray. There was also a good size box of imported chocolates from Japan. I know this because one of the girls I worked with was from Okinawa, Japan and she had some chocolate sent in a package from home and she gave me some 'cause she knows how much I like to try new things, and that was right up my alley. When she went home to visit one year, she had brought me three boxes back. They sell them in small sizes. Her name was Nyoko Oui. She used to bring in some of the most succulent sushi. I started eating that shit because Weezy turned Blair and I on to it after dating this half Chinese half black dude. He was beautiful but Weezy said his dick was too small. I used to laugh my ass off every time she talked about that dude. She said he was good to her but that she would eventually cheat on him because the sex was no good. I don't care what anyone says, that is a big part of a relationship. Not the whole part, but it's a large enough piece of the puzzle. I went into the bathroom that was set aside from the bedroom and opened the door to find a medium jacuzzi with a vanity sink and a sliding glass door shower. Blair would have loved this. The first thing he would have done was have his was with me in hot tub. He loved to have sex in new places. He loved hotels. He hated when he had to travel for different business conferences and things because he would have to stay in the hotel by himself. If he wasn't out with his friends, or out with someone who he knew, he would be calling me. I would fall asleep on the phone with him because if I hung up he would call back. I got the worst sleep when he wasn't around than I did when he was home. That nigga would wake me up in the middle of the night at the drop of a dime if his dick was hard. He didn't care what time it was. I would wake up to him inside me, and he was smooth about it too. After I got used to him doing that, every once in a while I'd stay sleep if he was quiet enough and soft enough, and that shit was a rare occasion where he was more tired than I was. If he know I had a long day or was about to face one he'd be quick about it.

I couldn't complain though 'cause I would cum too. I woke up several times having an orgasm. I was freaked out because at first I didn't know what was happening. That shit turned him on somethin' terrible. Anyway, the bathroom was nice. There were sienna marble floor tiles about three by three inches square covering the floor and the walls in the shower and behind the hot tub. There were some nice giant robes that looked like they'd swallow you up just like the carpet that I assume covers this whole hotel. I leave the bathroom and go sit on my queen size bed. This bed is decked out like it's fit for a queen. The big pillows are so inviting and comfy looking. I take off my air force ones and place my feet in that deep carpet. I felt like I was walking on air. I walked out into the living room where Weezy had already turned on the TV, kicked up her feet, and cracked a bottle of wine and was making little sandwiches with the crackers, meat, and cheese tray fixings. She had a glass waiting for me so I just plopped down next to her.

"Girl, this is some nice shit! It's amazing what a small change in tax bracket can get you!" Weezy said with a mouth full of grapes.

"I know. This is real nice. This is living!"

"But you know what's crazy? It gets even better than this. If Bill Gates had to stay in some shit like this, he'd be cursin' somebody out. This is how that man's roaches live."

I can't help but laugh. Weezy always got some crazy shit to say. We sat there till nightfall and drank two whole bottles of the wine. We were good and tipsy. We just sat there and talked about the room and different things and then Weezy jumped up.

"We didn't come down here to be sitin' in this room. I mean, it is nice as hell and I'm afraid to blink 'cause I might wake up in a cardboard box 'cause this is too good to be true" I'm laughing my ass off. "but we didn't come down here to watch TV because we can do that shit at home."

I was too tired. Traveling makes me sleepy. She was right though, we could watch TV at home. I wanted to go out though 'cause we could see the people in the streets moving and shaking and having a good time and we in the room getin' drunk.

"Weezy, girl I'm beat. I want to go out though but I won't make it too far before I'm ready to go to bed. I'm drunk and now I just want to shower and sleep."

I got to my room, undressed, and I know she's going to do the same, because as long as I've known Weezy, when she's tired she don't last long either. She'll try to fight it but she never wins. Not long after I get in my room I here her shut her door and I walk back over to mine, open it and yell "good night!" to her and she said good night back. I get in the shower and I don't know if it's because I'm drunk, but this water feels like liquid silk on my skin and the hot water seems to be telling my body something it's been waiting a long time to hear. After I got out, I lotioned with my favorite lavender lotion from Bath and Body Works, and I didn't even bother to put on PJ's. I open the curtains tonight and let the moonlight in. I pull back the sheets and rest for the first time, it seems, in a long time.

I wake to a strong beam of light shining right into my face. I roll over and look at the clock. It's eleven fifteen in the morning. I slept so good last night, I didn't want to get out of bed. I buzzed Weezy in her room from the call box on my nightstand to see if she was awake. I didn't get an answer and I didn't hear anything going on in the living room. It was dead quiet in that hotel room. It was so quiet in the room that I heard the bird on my windowsill fart. I grabbed the remote, I didn't notice the night before, and pressed the biggest button on it at the top and next thing I know the big wooden structure opens up that's in front of the foot of my bed and reveals a forty two inch color high definition television. Daaammmn! I missed some shit in here. I am going to have to explore this room a little more but not right now. I turn on the TV and it's on the cartoon channel, my favorite. After watching an hour of Courage The Cowardly Dog and SpongeBob, I get up and get myself together. I had found a note attached to my mirror when I took a bathroom break from Weezy saying:

"I tried to wake you up but you were sleeping like the dead so I just let you rest. Call my phone when you get up if I'm not back. Weezy."

I decided to call her after I got dressed and did my hair. It was about one forty in the afternoon and I was hungry. I called Weezy.

"Weez! Bitch you where you at?"

"Well look who woke from the damn dead. I went and did some looking around and then I came back to the hotel for lunch. I didn't want to wake you 'cause that sleep you caught last night was a good one it looked like!'

"Yeah, it was. I feel good and I'm dressed. I'm coming down." Before she can tell me where she sitting I hung up the phone and headed down stairs. I had on a cute yellow Liz Claybourne sundress and some yellow spaghetti strapped sandals. It goes nice with my almond mahogany skin tone. I get into the lobby and walk into the restaurant and I see Weezy as soon as I walk in. We had a nice breakfast and talked about the day's events. Weezy had grabbed a schedule of events from the concierge and was showing me different things we could do today. All I really wanted to do was go to Bourbon street and walk around there. I carried a knife 'cause they also say New Orleans isn't the happiest place on earth to be in certain places after dark. After eating, we gather ourselves and do some shopping and take in some of the sights and stare because there are some beautiful people down here. When it starts to get dark Weezy and I go back to the hotel and change into some evening clothes and hit the street. At about seven o'clock the streets are crawling with people just like we saw from our hotel window, only now there are a whole lot more people it seems downtown. The people are so nice. Weezy and I never have any trouble making friends with people and we fit in everywhere we go. So many people had bought us drinks that we barely made it outside to get to a cab. We partied hard. We were in and out of every club we laid our eyes on. I wasn't so drunk that I couldn't weld a gun though because I sure was carrying one under my arm in a holster in my jean jacket that I had to this Enyce jean shirt set. I would have fucked some shit up out here if they wanted to act up in those streets. I didn't tell Weezy I had it 'cause she really didn't do guns like that. Day after day we would shop and night after night we would party and drink. In four days I think we drank enough liquor to kill our livers three times over. We were the perfect tourists. We made more and more friends and hung out with the locals and other people from out of town every night. Everything was great and smooth until one particular night Weezy and I hit the street. I think it was our fifth or sixth night there or so, and again we were drinking. We were so drunk we couldn't remember our names and we decided to go get some tattoos. I got a tattoo of a ying yang sun and moon on my back. Weezy and I hadn't smoked any weed since I had been here and while I was getting my tattoo Weezy was standing outside talking to a guy she used to see in college. His name was Ronald Mooris, or Mr. Ring-a-ding to Weezy 'cause that man always knew how to hit her spot so she told me while she whispered drunk in my ear. She was breathing so hard on me I thought she was going to throw up on me which, I would have had to fuck her up for and it didn't surprise me when a few moments later she said she was going to stay with him for the rest of the night. I wasn't hatin' so I told her to have a good time and be safe and to call me when she reached her destination. When I said that to her she looked at me like she was crazy.

"Okay mom! I thought I left my mother in Jersey!"

"Yeah bitch if some shit happens to you I gonna be the first one you call so just give me a call and let me know you okay, please."

"Okay girl, I'll call you. I'll be fine. What about you? You want me to stay with you? I'll stay!"

"No Weez, go ahead and have fun. One of us should."

"Simone, that's what I'm talking about girl. We are on vacation and we are a little richer than we used to be, have good jobs, and we're in the prime of our lives. You've mourned enough! I loved Blair too, but he is gone from this world. He would want you to be happy." And with that Weezy hugged me and walked out. I thought about what she said and I just couldn't do it. I think Blair was the only man for me. I have never looked at another man since him. No one has moved me enough to sleep with them either. I just can't bring myself to sleep with someone and it not mean anything. My physical satisfaction has been taken beyond the flesh since I met Blair. It's all in my mind and only Blair knew how to reach it and when you've been that high off of love it's hard to come down and settle for something less. I'd feel like I was disrespecting him if I started fucking with some "no name." Especially if he couldn't make me cum like Blair did I'd probably kill him for wasting my time and his. I'm not going to set myself up for failure. Not long after Weezy leaves someone comes into the tattoo parlor, selling weed. I bought a twenty-dollar bag. Another dude waiting to get a tattoo rolled one up and went outside to smoke. When he came back fifteen minutes later he was fucked up and I knew that shit was going to be good. What Weezy said really rocked me and I guess it showed because the guy that was waiting on his tattoo leaned over to me and said, "You look like you could use this more than me." I took it and my artist told me it was okay to smoke it if I wanted to. "No one wants to see a pretty woman so sad." The tat man said. I just sat and smoked. He gave me half a Dutch full of weed. He must have not been paying attention when I bought the dub bag. Either that or he was that fucked up that he just didn't want anymore 'cause not long after he was sleep in the chair. My tattoo was finally done and it burned light hell. He rubbed it with some A&D ointment and told me to apply it as many times as I can for the next week, and then two to three times a day or as needed for itching after that. He also instructed me to keep it covered for the next hour as he bandaged it. I was high as shit. I didn't realize how high I was until I tried to stand up. The alcohol buzz wore off when that pain shot up my back from the tattoo, but I was going to quickly replace what I had lost. I went to the gas station on the corner and bought a pint of Hennessy to wet my whistle. Why I did that, I don't know. Weezy called me as I was leaving the store, but in my buzzed state I didn't hear the phone ring right away while it was in my pocket. I tried to call her back but she was leaving me a message. That said;

"Hey girl, I don't know why you haven't answered the phone but Ronald and I are back at the room. You probably out at the club. Call me if you want me to come get you okay. If you're fine you don't have to call me, but be safe Mone okay. Bye girl!"

I opened the Henny and went to town. I was so high I felt like my skin was crawling, which then made me think this shit was laced with something because in all the years I've smoked I have never felt like this. I was just walking the streets drinking. It was still early. I was only one thirty in the morning on a Saturday. It might as well be one o'clock in the afternoon because the streets were still littered with as many people outside as there were early today. The only difference is that there's no sun. I was walking in and out of the crowd like a zombie. I was stoned and I had drunk half that bottle of Henny. I walked until nothing looked familiar to me anymore. The people started looking scary instead of happy. I stopped because there was no telling how far I'd walked. It was now three am and my Henny was almost gone. I sat on a step in front of an old building. If I had to shoot someone now I might hit four other people before I hit my objective. I was so drunk I couldn't get up. I sat and leaned up against the wall and kicked out my legs and sat there like I was waiting for death. All I could hear was Weezy's voice in my ear talking about Blair and I felt his kisses all over me and I thought about the way he made me feel inside and out. I couldn't see life without him, even now as I was living it. I didn't know if I was going to be able to make it another day let alone another year. I started crying and the sky started spinning and I could hear screaming in my head. My own screams is what I heard. I heard the scream my heart let out when I saw Blair dead on that table in bits and pieces when I had to identify his body and with that last thought I popped. I threw up. I threw up a lot. I threw up shit other people had eaten and passed out. Right before I reached unconsciousness I saw a face of a woman reaching her hand to me. I felt like I was living in a dream. I remembered being carried and then I remembered being undressed and sitting in a tub with hands all over me. I think I was being bathed and rubbed all over with oil or something because I could smell orange ginger at one point, which is my favorite massage oil. The hands weren't doing anything to hurt me, I was afraid but I was too drunk to do anything about it. I was mad at myself for getting into this situation and I knew Weezy is going to be, if not already, worried about me. I wonder if she called the cops? The last I remembered was the face of a woman and then the lights went out. I had dreams of devils and angels and I was fighting them all for Blair. And as I smote the last who challenged my love for Blair he appeared. He looked so good and I was covered in blood and bleeding from the heart but I was still standing. He walked over to me and grabbed the sword from my hand and said, "The fight is over now. Rest." I do as he says and walk toward the warm light that is shining on me from the distance. The light surrounds me and comforts me. As the light gets brighter I notice I am no longer walking through the battlefield but lying in a bed. I'm in a room that is not my own. The window is directly in front of the bed at the foot of the bed and the sun is shining right on me. Now I know where that warm feeling was coming from. When my eyes finally focus I look around the room. It's a nice size room and it appears to be clean and very neat. The only thing that looks a mess in the room is me. I notice the white linen sleeves on my arms and realize I'm not in my own damn clothes, which then makes me look around the room to see if I can find them. I also, too, realize that my head is thumping and when I reach up to touch it there is a small bandage just to the left of my eyebrow that seems to be giving me signs of tenderness. I see a clock on the wall that tells me that it's four thirty in the afternoon. I try to sit up but the pain from my head is making it very difficult to manage this feat but when I finally reach my desired eye level I lean back on the head board. When I finally came to my senses I remembered that gun. I remembered that I wasn't in Atlanta anymore, and realized that Weezy might be worried sick about me. I realized as fucked up as I felt I might have to whip somebody's ass today. This is a nice room though. Someone lives here with taste and class. The furniture in the room was stained a deep chocolate color. There were spider plants hanging high on both sides of the bed, and there was that orange smell again. It was nice. I heard birds outside and plants dance in the gentle breeze that tiptoed in the window. The bed was queen size and the whole bed set was a pearl bone that set off its chocolate frame very well. I wanted to leave but some part of me wanted to stay and rest. This place seemed quiet and untouched by the rest of the world so out into the land of sleep I drifted once more. When I awoke the next time the sun was a little lower in the sky and the room had become a little darker. I was still feeling somewhat banged up but my head felt better than it did the first time I rolled over. I sat up in the bed and removed the covers from over me. I was dressed in a white linen pair of pajamas but nothing else. I was nude under the clothes. Then the door opened.

"Oh, you're awake. How are you feeling?"

"No worse the wear for the tear." I say, not sure of what my next move is going to be.

In walks this vanilla complexed woman with brown curly hair, and a soft Jamaican accent. It was so soft that the untrained ear would have missed it. She was beautiful. I could tell she was tone because the tank top she was wearing showed me everything about her upper body's definition. She was carrying what seemed to be my clothes draped over her forearm. She also had on a pair of white linen pants that looked identical to the ones I was wearing. The pants hung so low that a centimeter more and her pussy would not be left to anyone's imagination. Even in the low light of the room I could see that her eyes were very lightly colored, which the lamp later revealed as being gray.

"Where am I?"

"You are a long way from home. I hope you don't mind but I went through your wallet to find out who the woman was that was passed out on my doorstep."

"Doorstep?" I say confused because the last thing I remembered was, well, I guess I can't remember! Ain't that a bitch! Until I woke up I thought this was all a bad dream but I guess fate wouldn't have it that way today. I need to start going to church more 'cause it's only because of God I didn't wind up in some trash bag cut up into bits and pieces but I wasn't out of the clear yet. I still didn't know who the woman was and if she had a crazy brother who she knew like to rape girls in her house or a basement where she kept people as pets. What I was thinking must have been written on my face 'cause she then told me about herself.

"Simone is it? All your things are here with your clothes." And she motioned to the chocolate frame recliner with bone colored material surrounding the cushions she was standing over draping my clothes over one of the arms.

"I washed them because you had thrown up all over yourself." I was embarrassed as shit when she said that. Even though my complexion doesn't allow for too many variations as far me getting lights or darks, I knew at that moment I turned a bright red. There was something about this woman I couldn't quite put my finger on.

"I'm sorry, let me introduce myself. My name is Wyheeda. Wyheeda Collone."

"How did I get here?"

"Well, I was on my way out to the twenty four hour mini-mart up the street and found you on the steps. I could tell you weren't from around here, especially wearing a gun in the proper holster and shit. Everybody that carries a gun down here wears them in their pants." She thought what she said was funny but I wasn't laughing. I just wanted to hear about how I was undressed and came to be in what appeared to be her bed. When she saw I wasn't too amused, she continued. "Anyway," she continued, "I saw the bottle of Hennessy you had mostly finished laying on the ground and if I didn't get you were drunk by that, the puddle of the throw-up on you and in front of you was a good give away. I could smell it as soon as I opened the door." I just looked down at the ground. I know I must have looked like those pissy bums I saw laying on the sidewalk while I was out last night. She continued. "I picked you up and carried you upstairs, throw-up and all," was she gonna let that shit go or what? "and laid you down in the hallway outside the bathroom so I could get your clothes off. I saw the gun and unloaded it and put it in a box." With that said she pointed to a box next to the clock on the nightstand. "I wasn't going to put you in my bed with all the stuff on you so I ran some water and put you in the tub, and the whole time you never even stirred."

"I don't know what to say. Thank you."

"You are quite welcome. I thought you'd be sleep for a while and I knew you'd at least want some fresh clothes to put on when you woke up. Are you hungry?" I didn't answer right away although my mouth was about to motion yes I stopped. I was going to tell her no but my stomach said otherwise. Before I could say no, my stomach growled like ten pit bulls. She smiled 'cause she new the deal and said, "It's no trouble, really." And before I could look like I wanted to say anything she was out the door and on her way to the kitchen I suppose. I got up and walked over to my clothes and grabbed my cell phone which had a full mailbox, all the messages from Weezy. "Girl where in the hell are you? When you get this message call me right back." That was the first message. I knew she wasn't worried until she got up the next morning and went running in my room and I wasn't there. Last night she probably thought I didn't come home to give her some pimp room. "Girl what are you doing? It might be too much to hope you met someone and finally got laid so good you can't wake up, but I know that didn't happen. Bitch give me a call and let me know what you're doing." That was the second. "Simone, are you okay? Call me girl because I'm getting worried about you. I'm about to call the cops if you don't call me in the next hour." That was the third message. She sounded a little scared but like she was trying to keep it together. "Simone, girl, please call me! I called the cops. Girl if you can just get somewhere to call me. Just let me know you're okay." She was crying. I couldn't listen to anymore so I called her right then and there.

"Simone!?" Weezy answered the phone.

"Yeah Louise, it's me."

"Girl where in the fuck have you been? I've been worried sick about you and you know they kidnap people down here and shit and then you up and be gone all night. I almost lost my mind when I woke up and you weren't here. Especially when the day started to end and I hadn't gotten so much as a message from you. Girl you worth too much money to be walking around here by yourself in a strange neighborhood. Are you alright? The cops told me you have to be missing for at least twenty four hours before you could be declared missing. And," I had to stop her because I thought she was going to have a nervous breakdown.

"I'm okay, I'm okay. I just got a little drunk and passed out on the sidewalk, but I'm alright."

"What the hell do you mean, 'on the sidewalk?'" I could just picture her face when she said that and I tried not to laugh because she was upset.

"I passed out on a woman's step and she took me in and cleaned me up, and put me to bed for the night. She took care of me."

"Who the hell is she?" Louise said frantically.

"I don't know, but she's real nice. I feel like I know her from somewhere!"

"Well what are you doing now?"

"I just woke up and she's making me breakfast."

"Breakfast?!" She said. I couldn't help but snicker this time. "What the hell is this bitch, Betty Crocker?"

"Girl stop. I gotta go. I'll call you when I get myself together to leave."

"Well where in the hell are you? I'll have a car from the hotel bring me to pick you up!"

"No, I'm fine. I'll tell you everything as soon as I get back and my phone will be on and nearby, so you can call at any time, okay?"

"Simone, I don't like this. Tell me where you are so I can come and get you." I couldn't tell her to come get me because I honestly didn't know.

"I don't actually know, but I'm fine. Trust me."

"Mone let me talk to her! Let me talk to her. I don't wanna have to kill that bitch!" I knew she was mad and worried but I couldn't stop laughing. I told her I wasn't going to let her talk to her and made Louise get off the phone. I told her to call me anytime she felt the need or that I would call if anything changed because I killed this woman in here for acting loony. I don't know karate, but I know cra-azee. After I hung up with her she called me right back and said,' I just wanted to make sure it was really on and that she wasn't making you say that.' I just hung up the phone and got myself together before leaving the room. I opened the door and walked out toward the balcony that overlooks the living room. To the left at the end of the hallway there is the bathroom of which I had the royal treatment I wasn't awake for, and to my left at the end of the hallway there is another room, which I think is a guest room because it's not as lived in looking as the other room. The bed was made real nice and there wasn't as much furniture either, but it was nice. It made me wonder though, why she put me in her bed and not in the guest room. Was I more than a guest? Anyway at the far end of the hallway there was another more smaller room that looked like an office. It, too, was also very nice. The door was wide open. I could see the black desktop Dell computer, some files, and some paperwork sitting on top of the desk. There was also a big picture hanging on the wall but I really couldn't see what that was though. I could see the whole down stairs from up here and it was a nice set up. I could tell she didn't have any kind of kids running through here because that beige couch would have been done for. I don't even trust myself around something like that. The ceilings were very high and so were the windows but you could sit in them. She had a beautiful candle set up going on around the working fireplace and she gave a whole new meaning to the word entertainment system. She had a hug flat screen TV just like the one at the hotel. I'm missing out. Maybe when I go back home I'll buy one. Blair and I never watch too much TV for too long. I mean, we watched cartoons and I watched a movie here and there and he would watch sports from time to time when the games were on for basketball and football, but other than that the TV was off. If it was on sometimes we'd be sitting there, but we be watching each other. Blair like to play games. He would time himself to see if he could make me cum by eating me out before the next commercial break. He succeeded many times, so that's why I had no problems. I walked down the stairs and I was starting to smell what my chef was cooking. She had pulled out a whole bunch of food to cook. I was just hoping for some eggs and bacon or a bowl of cereal or some shit like that but Wyheeda pulled out some chicken that looked like she had marinating it over night or something. I guess it was about right though because it was about diner time and I hadn't eaten since early last night and I had thrown up everything I ever ate apparently last night as well. When she noticed me come down stairs she turned and smiled, and kept on about what she was doing. She had made me a sandwich and it was sitting on the counter. "That'll hold you till dinner, 'cause I know you don't have anything in your stomach." She said and pushed the plate with the turkey and cheese sandwich with mustard and pickles over to me and poured me a glass of guava juice on ice, my favorite! It was odd to me how comfortable I felt. I thought I was losing my mind for a second because you know black folks don't do shit like this, but for some reason I was changing the rules today! I said thank you and took the sandwich. I started to get up to wash my hands but she pointed to the napkin, which was actually a moist towelette, and I wiped my hands. This bitch had everything so I wanted to know, ev-er-ything about her. I couldn't help but be curious. I watched her move around the kitchen with grace and ease, and the smells she was creating during her cooking dance were magnificent. She didn't say much and neither did I. I felt, for one reason or another, that there was no reason for me to talk. There was a comfortable silence, and I enjoyed that. The silence didn't last long because Weezy was trying to reach out and touch a sista so I answered the phone.

"Yes, Weezy?" I said calmly so as not to alarm her.

"Are you okay? What time are you coming back?"

"I don't know. Why-hee-da, is making dinner, I suppose, and I'm invited to stay." I say still speaking calmly. Whyheeda turns around and smiles.

"If that's a friend of yours they are more than welcome to come as well if they're worried about you." That was so nice of her. I know she did it to make me more comfortable too, and before Whyheeda could finish the whole thought, Weez had a piece of paper and pen ready to take down the woman's address. Whyheeda took the phone and talked briefly as I sat there worried about what Weezy might ask her. I do know Louise asked her how I wound up in her care, because Whyheeda laughed as she looked at me and said," It's a long story. I'll tell you all about it to both of you as soon as I get you seated at my table." Whyheeda gave Louise instructions on how to get to her dwelling and then she hung up and continued with dinner.

"If you want you can go take a shower and freshen up. Dinner won't be ready for another hour or so, and all your clothes are clean." I had forgotten I didn't have anything on under these pj's, so I took her up on her offer. I drank the last of my juice and headed up the steps. She told me where to find a washcloth and towel, and I was on my way. Her bathroom was niiicccee. The last time I had seen a deep tub like that was in the Four Seasons Hotel where Blair and I would go to get away sometimes. They filled up in like sixty seconds. I sat on the edge of the tub and thought about the nights he'd run me a warm bath and bathe me on those nights my cramps were bothering me more than others, or just to have a reason to touch me, as if he needed one, but he'd do it. He'd massage my back and during these baths would be the only time he would refuse me. He let me have him one time during a bath but never again because he said my bath times were about me and me only, and that his needs would have to wait. That shit used to make me so mad. Even if I was the one advancing he still would tell me no. I would want it so bad after that my pussy would start to hurt. I remember one time I ripped his shirt clean off of him and he still told me no. I could see his dick was hard through those sweatpants he used to wear around the house but he still would say no. He enjoyed seeing my flesh submerged in water. I became a star for him to gaze at and admire. It was also during these moments the love for me really showed in his eyes, as if he was seeing me for the first time. We made some good love. The strokes that man used to give me used to have me in my car crying on my way to work thinking about the evening past. When he wanted to be rough, he would fuck the shit out of me. He would hurt me sometimes, not in a bad way though. I loved to surrender my body to him because I knew he could handle it. No real woman wants a weak man, and Blair was everything but weak. I like how the shower was separate from the tub. She had a nice place and I wondered what she did for a living and how she did it. That hot water felt good on my face and down my back. I imagined the water drops were Blair's finger tips running down my body. I wish he could just reach out and touch me. I thought about the dream I had last night or whenever I was sleeping in my drunken state. That's how I know I was drunk because I was in a dream fighting and shit. I'm not a violent person but used to wrestle with him when I was drunk. He thought it was funny. I felt like in the dream he was telling me to let him go. I mean, he took the sword from me and told me I was done. He watched me walk away. Some part of me didn't want to believe it even though I knew it was true. I believe in my dreams. They show me things. Next thing I know there was a knock on the door.

"Are you alright?" Whyheeda said.

"I'm fine. That alcohol still has a small grip on me though." She laughed. "But, other than that I'm good." I said in a low voice.

"Well, you can use the lotion and stuff in my room if you want. I have a new deodorant if you want to use it. I'll sit it out for you." I wonder if she slept in that bed with me?

I acknowledged her offer and back to cooking she went. I felt good after I got out that shower. I sat in the room and looked around for a moment. It was very well put together. I liked her style. I really looked at it this time 'cause when you first wake up in an unknown room, the first thing you do is look for the way out, so needless to say I didn't really pay too much attention to everything around me. If it wasn't moving it wasn't important. Whyheeda also had a nice candle set up in the far corner of the room on the little iron candle holder. It was like stair steps. The towers were different heights on which peach and cinnamon candles sat upon them, which were also now lit. It smelled real nice. I looked on her dresser and saw she had a simple collection of scents and lotions like me. I walked over to the dresser and found some not so strong smelling lotion and applied it to my entire body as always. I don't do ashy, but almost fainted when I saw a most familiar bottle sitting in the front. It was the same one Blair used to wear. I could never pronounce the name of it but I loved it, and there it was larger than life. Before I knew it I had sprayed it on myself. Immediately I was turned on. I felt like I was on fire. I wanted sex. It's been two years since I had a man next to me and I was feeling real primal. I wanted sex in any way it could get to me. The wind started blowing softly in the room and

I felt like there was someone in there watching me. I gathered myself when I heard the doorbell ring. It was Weezy. I finished dressing and came downstairs. She was relieved to see that I was okay and gave me a big long hug. Whyheeda just smiled at the reunion of the two friends.

"Girl I'm so glad you are okay." Weezy blurted out real loud after our hug. I knew they had already introduced themselves but I did it again, it was polite.

"I'm good girl." I felt weird though. I didn't know this woman from a can of paint and we were about to eat at her house for diner after she picks me up off the sidewalk and shines me up like a new penny. It was weird!

"Whyheeda has taken good care of me." Before I could say another word she said, "Please, call me Why.", And I do mean like the word "why". The dinner Why made was wonderful. She made baked marinated chicken, wild Irish red potatoes, and string beans. I don't know what kind of wine it was but it was delightful. We sat and laughed like we had known each other for years. She told us both about herself and what she did for a living and how she cared for me and my drunk self.

"I couldn't just leave a woman on my step looking half dead. She looked too clean, aside from the vomit, and well dressed to be one of these crazies out here. I damn sure wasn't going to leave her to them. I think she had just passed out when I came to the door. I was somewhat scared at first because she had a gun, but she had the license for it in her wallet so I thought she couldn't be too dangerous because someone who starts trouble wouldn't have something like that. I knew it was just for protection. Especially if you're going to pass out in the crazy streets of New Orleans!" I smiled kind of embarrassed.

"I'm glad you found her before someone up to no good did." Weezy said relieved. "I was going crazy. I thought someone grabbed her up and did some down south voodoo on her or something." I laughed, but she was serious as hell.

Whyheeda told us a lot about herself. She was born in Florida and she was married, but she found him cheating on her after three years so she left him and went on her way. She is a twenty-nine year old doctor and she is out of work for a little while because she had her appendix taken out. She'd been out for a month and couldn't wait to go back to work. I wonder, if you're a doctor, do you get to pick what doctor friend does your operation? I wasn't going to ask her that stupid question though. She also modeled a little while she was in high school. I could believe that. She was really exotic looking. She moved to New Orleans when she was about three with her parents. Her mother was Creole and her father was Puerto Rican. Like I said, she was beautiful. She seemed to light up a room. Whyheeda never had any kids. She had been pregnant a year into her marriage but she lost the baby because she had gotten pneumonia. She was six months into the pregnancy when it happened. She's been on her own for three years now and is in no rush to change it. I could see the pain and hurt in her face as she spoke about the events in her past. I knew what she was going through. To lose someone you love, no matter how you lose them, is hard. Blair was taken from me, and Whyheeda left her ex and sometimes that's even worse. I guess that's the way she dismisses her anger and frustrations by just "working" it out, literally. I enjoyed her company. After dinner Weezy and I helped her clean up. We filled the dishwasher up, and the dishes that didn't fit I washed by hand. I thanked her for her hospitality and told her that if there was anything that she needed to call me. We exchanged numbers and all other information, and back to the hotel we went. Louise and I talked about that shit the whole way back. I walked for a long ass time last night. It took us twenty minutes to get back in the car. No wonder I slept like the dead. When we got back into the hotel I felt like I was back on safe grounds. I changed out of my clothes and put on my pajamas and sat in the living room. Weezy came bursting out of her room a few moments later.

"Bitch, don't you ever scare me like that again!" Her hands were play choking me. "You scared the shit out of me. You know you my only real friend in this world and "B" was like the brother I never had. I can't lose both of you now. You the only real close family I got." B was what she called Blair sometimes.

"Scared you?! I was the one who woke up in some strange place. I didn't know where the hell I was. I thought someone kidnapped me and took me to another country or something. She had a nice apartment for that neighborhood she was in." I said with a shocked look because of what could have happened had she not pulled me into her palace.

"I know right! Her shit was nice. I thought I was going to have to snatch you up outta there. When I saw that neighborhood, and the outside of her building I really thought about skipping dinner and going to the store to buy her a can of Raid as a housewarming gift. I don't care how long she lived there!" I laughed so hard when she said that, that I choked on the apple iced tea I was drinking.

"Yo, it wasn't till we stepped outside that I got a little scared. I mean all the damn crack heads and shit moving around like roaches and shit. Huggy bear the pimp on the corner in that grape purple suit! Girl, and it had a feather too. You know what bugged me the most though, was the fact that he was as black as night and fat. He looked like a big bruise standing on that corner." Now Weez is laughing. "I want to know how she got such a nice apartment in such a beat area. I mean, I done been in the hood and have never seen a place like that in it."

I decided to go to bed even though I wasn't tired. I slept most of the day at Whyheeda's place and I just wanted to be still for the rest of the evening. Weezy's friend Ronald called her on the late night, and wanted to see her. I think it was about one thirty, two o'clock. I was up when Weezy came in my room and told me she'd be in the lobby for a while and might be back with some company. I ordered Land of the Dead on the TV on one of the channels you can order movies from and popped some popcorn. Now I don't know what made me do it, but

I picked up my phone and dialed a number I probably shouldn't have dialed, but I couldn't stop myself, or maybe I just didn't want to. We'll never know. I called Whyheeda. I figured she'd be up because she was up when she found me on her doorstep and in the conversation at diner I found out she was a night owl like me. The whole time the phone was ranging, I was nervous but I didn't know what for. I was hoping to get an answering machine, but to my surprise she answered.

"Hello?" She said in a sweet calm sleepy voice.

"Hey Why. It's me, Simone. Did I wake you?"

"No. I was just sitting here watching a movie and eating some popcorn." I smiled.

"Me too. Listen, I just wanted to call and let you know Louise and I made it home okay, and to say thank you for everything. I didn't want to bother you." And here's where the script really began to flip.

"No, no. Bother me anytime you feel the need. I'll be here." I didn't know what to say.

"Thanks." I paused for a moment. "What are you watching?"

"House on the Haunted Hill. I love scary movies."

"Me too. My fiancé and I used to watch scary movies that came out." I said sadden a little, and she could tell.

"You were engaged? What happened?" She said, sounding more awake than before. I paused again then spoke.

"Yeah, I was. He was in a car accident. I didn't even get to say goodbye." I got quiet for a minute. I could tell she was waiting for me to say something. "I'm okay though. It's been two years."

"Sometimes it takes a lifetime, but you have to know when to stop fighting within yourself in order to move on. It's okay to mourn, but it can either be healthy or harmful." I appreciated that coming from a complete stranger. What's even funnier was when she brought up that fighting within yourself stuff. I thought about that dream I had at her place. Blair told me the same thing in the dream. You know, that my fight was over.

"I'm sorry. I didn't call to sadden you with my past." She interrupted me.

"Tell me then, what did you call for? Honestly!"

"I don't know. Sometimes it feels better to talk things over to someone with a fresh mind. See how things look from someone on the outside who hasn't been exposed to the insanity I guess." That was half honest. The real reason I called I didn't even want to admit to myself.

"Yeah, you're right. Someone who can't judge you from knowing too much." We talked a while longer about where I was from and more things that we had in common. We were on the phone about, oh I don't know, forty minutes! It was late and I missed most of the movie.

"We'll, I've bored you long enough. I'm gonna get some sleep." I wasn't even sleepy. I just didn't want her to know how much I enjoyed talking to her.

"You've been far from boring. If you don't have any plans, do you want to come over for a late dinner tomorrow Simone? We can do it night owl style!" And for the second time in my life I said yes faster than white people sunburn at the beach in summer. I know she noticed because she didn't even have her response ready yet. She didn't say anything though. She just said, "Good, see you tomorrow at nine." When I got off the phone I found myself smiling uncontrollably. Like someone told me a dirty little secret or something. I didn't go to sleep that night until four thirty, five o'clock after getting off the phone with her so I would be wide awake at dinner. Bright and early the next morning Weezy came into the room jumping on the bed with a big smile on her face. I wasn't as enthused as her 'cause I had only been sleep for four hours. This early morning jumping around thing was no doubt due to Mr. Ring-a-ding, which means Weezy got some last night. She climbed in the bed and turned on the TV as if I weren't even in there sleeping. "Girl get up!" she said, switching channels.

"Girl, I just went to sleep. I'm tired. Get out." As if I said nothing, she asked about breakfast and where we were going to eat it.

"Why don't we eat breakfast downstairs again? The food was pretty good. I'm in the mood for some pancakes!" I ignored her and tried to drift back to sleep. "When are you getting up?" I ignored her again. "I'ma call Ronald back and see if he wants to meet me for breakfast." I guess he agreed 'cause what seemed like only moments later I heard her walking out the door. I rolled over and saw a note on the nightstand that said, "Call my phone when you get up and let me know what you're doing." It was eleven forty five in the morning so I took my black ass right back to sleep. When I woke next and I looked at the clock, it was three o'clock. I got up and was hungry as hell. I ordered room service because for some reason I didn't want to leave this room until I had to later on for dinner. I called Weezy to see what she was doing and I got an answering machine so I left a message. In doing that I also checked my own messages. I had one from my business manager asking about a shipment of lumber coming in and how he got it at a good price and a better quality. I had one from my mother, asking how I was doing and how the vacation was going. She was also thanking me for the dozens of roses I had sent to the house to her and my father just to say I love you. You never know when people are going to come and go in this world so it is important to let them know you love them all the time, and I know that Blair went out of this world knowing that if no one else loved him, I did. He knows I would have slit my throat to save his neck. There were a few more messages from some friends and co-workers wondering when I was coming home so I could tell them about my trip. It was like they all got together and decided to call one after the other. The last message I got was the one that made me smile inside and out. It was Whyheeda.

She was like, "Hey Simone. You don't have to return this phone call. I was just calling to tell you that you don't have to dress up for dinner. Just be as comfortable as you want when you come over. Call me if you're canceling okay. I hope you don't though, but if you do I understand. Bye." The sound of her voice was comforting. I couldn't wait to go see her. For some strange reason, she moved me. It was now five thirty. I had worked out in the gym down stairs and got a massage that was heaven. I had some old one hundred year old looking woman with four good teeth and slightly balding, give me the best massage I'd had in a long time. The shit was sooo good I went to sleep on the table. I was in there for about an hour. I felt so rejuvenated, just like they said in the brochure up stairs in the room. I felt brand new. For some reason or other the day just seemed a little bit brighter. When I came back upstairs it was six forty five. I had plenty of time to get ready and pick up some wine and flowers for dinner. I would have picked up some dessert from this wonderful bakery Weezy and I stumbled upon the other day, that had some of the most heavenly pastry I'd ever had the pleasure to tease my palate with. It was pricey as hell but it was well worth it. They had this cheesecake cupcake that was good enough to make you spend a paycheck buying one after the other. I was almost sick I ate so many. I got in the shower and the water seems to be playing with my body. It was like it was touching me instead of just rinsing me. When I got out and dried off, it was as if my towel was just a little softer than before. It was like my senses were running wild. I was truly awake. I lotioned and then put on my favorite oil. I don't know what it was about this oil, but it just made me want to touch myself. It smelled that good to me. Not many people know about it, so when I walked into a room heads automatically turned my way. It wasn't a strong smell, but after I physically left the room I would still be there, in a manner of speaking. She said comfortable, so I got out the most comfortable thing I could think of. I had a heather gray Hilfigure sweat suit. It was a pair of sweatpants and a jacket with a hood that had Tommy across the bottom. I put on a new matching pair of bra and panties from Victoria's Secret that was also gray. I put on a white wife beater and a pair of fresh Airforce Ones. I put my hair in a ponytail and put a little curl in it and I was done. She said comfortable so I was going to give that a new meaning. The sweat suit was nice and baggy. It was nice and soft on the inside and it felt like I didn't have anything on and I liked that feeling. I was nice and loose. I had a nice massage and I was relaxed, so the last thing I wanted to do was confine my body to some tight clothes. "Be comfortable," was the best thing Whyheeda could have said to me. I called to the concierge and had them pick up some nice flowers and a nice bottle of wine, no more than two hundred dollars. I forgot I could get them to get that kind of stuff. That gave me even more time. They know where to get that stuff. I told them to just put it in the car when it arrived because I would be leaving with the items and they gladly honored my request. At seven fifty I was on my way. I looked at the streets filled with people smiling and laughing. I felt like I was in a movie and I was watching life through a big screen. Everything seemed to be going in slow motion but I thought it was nice. Time slowed down for me for once. When I arrived at her place, I had forgotten how frightening her apartment building looked. When you first walk in there it is an abandoned warehouse floor with a freight elevator way in the back. It was big. There were cars parked in here though so I guess it was their parking lot. The elevator looked new compared to everything else. It really separated the old from the new. The inside of it was nice. The first floor of the building actually started three floors up. It was like entering a new world when I got off at the fifth floor. The hallway was carpeted wall to wall. The apartment numbers on the doors looked like twenty four karat gold. When I got to her door I was nervous as hell. I could smell the enchanting aromas evading the air under my nose. I listened for a moment because I heard a very familiar voice singing. It was Bares Hammond playing in the background. I knocked on the door and within moments she answered. She looked even prettier than I remembered. As soon as she opened the door the wind carried the scent of her body past my face. She was wearing that colon, the one I had put on that day I left here, the one that Blair used to wear. My nipples got hard instantly thinking of it. Good thing I had on that sweat jacket or I might have been a little embarrassed. She reached out and hugged me and said, "I'm glad you could make it!" Yeah, so was I. She ushered me in and she followed. The apartment smelled really nice. It was a light musk smell with a touch of lavender it seemed. I was instantly relaxed because of it. I sat down on the couch and made myself at home in this place from which I recently had already become acquainted with. Dinner smelled wonderful. I sat down on the couch that had the look of hand crafted all over it and put my mind at ease. A glass of wine was brought to me with a small saucer of fruits and cheeses. I could still feel her arms around me from our embrace just moments ago. She came in and sat down on the couch across from me. She also had a glass of wine and kicked her feet up on the coffee table. She had on a pair of sandals and her toes were perfectly done. Whyheeda was wearing a red pair of Victoria Secrets flannel pajama bottoms. I knew that they were new because I had just seen them in the new catalog for the month, and she had on a too small undershirt that fit just right. Yes, we were comfortable. I watched her every move without watching her, if you know what I mean. For some strange reason, I wanted to know about her, in every meaning of the word. I wanted to know what made her tick. Why she picked me up off the curb, or why she went that extra step to clean me up. I wanted to know. Her hair was back in a clip with some hair along the side of her face. I listened to her speak and the way she said my name. I listened to the way she hummed when she stirred the gumbo. I listened and watched. By the time I had finished the glass of wine dinner was ready.

"I love a well prepared meal, but when you dress up all the time sometimes you just want to be cozy, you know?" I knew just what she meant. I would fix gourmet meals for Blair and but we would eat in our pjs or sometimes naked or in our underwear. Hell, we were in our own damn house. The table setting was beautiful and prior to her setting it I asked if she needed help and she refused. Why said, "You are my guest and you will be treated as such. You won't be lifting a finger tonight. Girl, relax!" So I did. Over diner I had told her about

Blair and how madly in love I was with that man and how I still am. I told her about my life and everything to the point where we were sitting on her balcony talking over some gourmet coffee with a splash of rum. It warmed me. I talked like I was being interviewed and she asked questions as such. She enjoyed me telling her about how Blair and I met. There are only a few people who know the entire story as it is told from head to toe, and only my closest friends and family know that one look from that man made me drop my drawls like a hoe in a room full of money. I told her about the love we made and the many places we made it. I told her how I was crushed when he died and even the dream I had while in her care from the night before. It felt so good to tell someone. It was like I had to get it all off my chest. I hadn't really spoken to anyone about the whole thing since it happened. Weezy was there going through it with me and my other friends, well, they just knew of the love I'd lost. I never really sat down and told anyone how it made me feel inside, and talking to Whyheeda about it seemed to rest what little of a soul I had left. I felt dead when Blair left. Dead! Whyheeda just listened, comforting me 'cause I was now crying an ocean of tears.

"Simone, the important thing is that he did all he could for you while he was here, and you know he loved you very much, and he didn't suffer. That's the important thing. I know you miss him, but there will be others. God never shuts one door without opening another." Whyheeda wiped the tears streaming down my face with her hand. By now she was sitting next to me with her arm around my shoulders. Man, she smelled good. Her body heat felt like fire. I hadn't been that close to another human being in a long time. Weezy and family don't count. Well, Weezy is like family, so I guess she really don't count at all. I guess, no one really knew except God. I closed my eyes and let the smell of her awaken memories of love lost and the road less traveled by, and let her feed my appetite for affection. She was rubbing my back in long slow strokes. It felt so good. I don't know what came over me. I lifted my head up out of hands and looked her in her pretty eyes. I looked at her lips. I looked at her breast, and I looked at her arms. I looked at everything that set her apart from everyone else. I looked at her and she looked back at me. She wiped the hair that was laying across my right eye and rested her hand on my neck with her thumb grazing the lining of my jaw. I couldn't hide the satisfaction her touches were giving me any longer. I needed air. I gathered my thoughts and walked over to the edge of the balcony overlooking the quiet spooky neighborhood. I could see the lights from the boulevard off in the distance. The parties seemed to go on as usual without a care in the world. The pimps and hoes worked their corners and johns. It was about eleven forty five on a Friday night and I looked up and saw a shooting star in the sky. Weezy and I were leaving on Sunday and I now didn't want to go. I wiped a few tears from my eyes and watched the life being lived below me. I turned around and looked at Whyheeda. Her sitting in that moonlight gave her a silver lining. She looked so pure, so beautiful. She had a few tears in her eyes because she too knows what it is to love and lose. It was then I realized I wanted her. I wanted her bad. All night she had said and did the right things. Whyheeda was beautiful in so many ways. She was hypnotizing to me. I was stuck in a trance that was broken by the ring of my cell phone. I walked into the living room and retrieved my phone from my bag. It was Weezy.

"Hey girl! Where are you? I'm still out but I called the room, that's how I know you weren't there." She said, waiting for an explanation.

"I'm fine. I'll be home in a little bit." I said. I guess that wasn't enough though.

"Well, I'm outside this bar called Little Blue, and I'll be on my way to the room soon to change into some evening wear because Ronald wants to take me to this place down here called the Red Snapper. You should come down and meet me. Where are you? I could come get you if you want me too!" She said wanting any small hint as to where my location was.

"I'm at Why's. She made dinner and invited me to join her, so I came." Lord knows I wanted to mean that in a different way. "She made gumbo and it was good." I said grinning because Whyheeda was now standing in the doorway smiling at my compliment.

"Simmy you good?" I had only heard Louis call me that a handful of times and it was usually when she was drinking or when she was worried.

"I'm fine. I'll call you as soon as I get back to the room. I'll have the car service pick me up. Anyway, I need to be asking about you. You the one hanging out with some strange man! I don't have to fuck no one up do I? You been spending a lot of time with this dude." Weezy was laughing. "He must be showing you a damn good time!"

"Don't even act like I've been keeping you in the dark. You haven't been still long enough to meet him. I called after breakfast but I think you were still sleep. I was going to bring him up to meet you but I know what you get like when you want your sleep, and I knew you were still in the room because to you it was still early!" She went on to say.

After debating with her for a few more moments we put each other's minds at ease and hung up. Whyheeda was putting the teacups away and clearing the table outside and I followed with the remaining dishes. She had run some nice hot soapy water to sit the dishes in. I told her I'd better be getting on my way and she acknowledged. As I soaped the saucers in the dishwasher, she came up behind me and put the dishes in that had earlier presented the cheese and fruit into the sink. Her breasts were on my back and the smell of her hair was on my lips. She reached up and put a grape in my mouth and walked away as if it were nothing. She was driving me crazy. I had to get out of there. She might think I was the hell crazy. All she wanted was to invite me to dinner, not get my panties wet. That woman wasn't thinking about me, she was just being nice. I mean she has seen me naked and I could have died on her front step, so she kind of saved my life. How shy could I be? Here I am drooling over her and frankly I don't know why. I had been in the hospital before and had women come onto me, even in my depressed state that I was in, and there were tons of beautiful women waiting on me hand and foot so why was she special? Why did I want her? I had to get the hell out of there and fast. I have just come to the conclusion that I want to fuck a woman and I'm standing in that same woman's kitchen washing her dishes and she has no idea I feel the way I do. I haven't had sex in so long my pussy is aching and there is nothing I can do about it. Next thing I know there is a sharp pain in my hand, and runs up my arm. I pulled my hand out of the water and there was a small cut on the back of my right ring finger. I called Whyheeda and asked her if she had a band aid, which is a dumb question to ask a doctor because she probably had a fully equipped emergency room in a closet or something. The thought of it made me laugh to myself. She came over and saw the cut, grabbed my hand and walked me to the bathroom. She turned on the water, removed the towel and placed my hand under it, and told me to sit tight. It wasn't hurting much before but it was starting to sting more now. Whyheeda came back with her first aid kit. Again she stood behind me and washed it with some kind of antibacterial soap that was orange and smelled real nice.

"What happen?" She asked, concerned.

I told her how I was daydreaming and didn't realize I had even done it.

She laughed and said, "Happens to us all!" We both laughed.

Without words she continued to rub and clean until the bleeding slowed. I cut myself pretty good. I didn't need stitches but I'd have to keep it taped up for a while. I was loving the attention. She stood close to me once more, just the way she did at the kitchen sink. Her whole body was rested against mine. She was a little shorter than I was so she kind of leaned over on shoulder to see and she rested her cheek on my arm. My whole body felt awake. I wanted to kiss her so bad but I tried to continue to seem unmoved by the intimacy of this interaction. She turned off the water and grabbed a towel and dried the wound that had now clearly revealed itself. It was a nasty little cut but I was going to live. I sat down on the toilet as I continued to dry my hand. I watched her. I watched her every waking move. Her eyes were so lovely and she smelled so good. I wanted her to try to give me a bath now that I was awake. I wanted her hands all over. I don't know what the hell is wrong with me. By the time I came back to my scenes she was done. My finger was all taped up and ready to go. She could tell I wasn't too thrilled with what was happening. "Don't worry. It'll hurt in the morning but it will be fine." She said trying to ease my discomfort, but it wasn't that. It wasn't hurting or the pain that was soon to come that had me displeased. It was the simple fact that she was done touching me. Her hands were so steady and calm. I can tell she was a good surgeon. It almost seemed graceful, like her hands danced with mine and she was leading. Whyheeda put all the extra band-aids and gals in the box and I stood up. I said thank you and we headed back down the stairs. Before I could say another word, Whyheeda made me an offer I couldn't refuse.

"Listen, I know it's late but I picked up a few movies, and I know you like scary movies, so I was wondering if you wanted to stay and watch some." I couldn't say no. One, because I obviously hadn't overstayed my welcome and two, I am a sucker for a good scary movie. She had rented "The Exorcism Of Emily Rose." I just couldn't refuse. We made some popcorn, turned off the lights, and planted ourselves down in the living room in front of the big plasma flat screen, which I definitely have to get up on when I go home, and put in the tape. That movie scared the shit out of both of us. We sat so close together she was almost in my lap. She normally didn't watch that kind of stuff, but every now-and-again she would. I was all eyes though. That movie had us both shaking and we were only half way through, but the movie's viewing came to a screeching halt when the scene came where the guy had awakened in the middle of the night to find her laying on the floor. Whyheeda put her head in my neck and asked me to turn it off 'cause it scared her so bad. By now we were on the same couch. I stopped the movie and she still didn't move. Her body was half way draped in my lap and hugging me. She smelled so good I found myself enjoying her embrace without me even knowing it. I was rubbing her back and smelling her hair, it was nice, and before I knew it she was relaxing in my arms. Her hands were rubbing the back of my neck, and her nose and lips wandered around my neck. She raised her face slowly and rubbed it against mine 'till she reached my lips and kissed me. Time stopped, the wind was still, and sound was no more. All that existed at that moment was that kiss. My heart began to beat so fast that she stopped kissing to place her hand on it. "It's okay, everything's alright." She said, and she kissed me again. Whyheeda stood to her feet and knelt down between my legs on the floor in front of the couch. She pulled me to the edge of the couch where we embraced and kissed again, while she lifted my wife beater and bra to release my breast from their confinement. She lifted the shirt to glimpse my nipples before she began putting them in her mouth. My breasts are a weakness I've had all my life. I had become putty in her hands. She stood me up and took my hand and led me up to the bedroom. Neither one of us spoke. There was nothing to say. We knew what we wanted and that was that. Once in the bedroom she undressed me, removing the undershirt and bra that sat atop my breast. She removed my sweatpants and panties. She could tell that the level of excitement had reached a high because of the moisture gathered on my pubic hair. She laid me down on the bed and stared at me standing up. It is there that she undressed and lowered her body to mine. She was so warm and soft, and her movements seemed effortless. She rested her body on top of mine and kissed me in the most passionate way. Her movements were slow and steady, and her body rolled over mine like a wave of water. I felt like summer in fall and wet where it was dry. I felt high at the lowest point and I felt bliss in the land of the wicked. She gently grinded her body into mine and I felt so right in more ways than one, and this feeling began to grow in the core of my love. It got bigger and bigger until.... My whole body tightened and my teeth clenched.

My body jumped and slight convulsions began to occur. I hadn't let loose like that in quite some time. I felt so drained that my body went limp. Whyheeda was holding me close and kissing me very tentatively on my lips. Her kisses hung in my mind like clouds in the sky. She reached over and turned out the light, and we stopped right where we started and slept. I arose in the morning to the smell of blueberry waffles, coffee, and an omelet. For a second I didn't move. What the hell was I thinking? Why in the hell did I do that? Is she going to want more from me? I felt sick to my stomach. She was a great person, but this just wasn't me. I don't know where my mind was. Nah, she'll be cool about it. She's pretty grounded. I got up and sat on the edge of the bed. I didn't want breakfast. This is the one time in my life I was hoping that the food wasn't for me. I got up and went into the bathroom to wash up. I stood and looked at my face in the mirror after dousing it with some water. I noticed a smear of blood going down my nose. There were no cuts on my face so I flipped my hand over and there was blood on my fingers. I looked at where I had been resting my hand and there was some dried blood that we must have missed last night on the side of the sink. I'm glad that's what it was because I thought I was going to lose my mind for a minute. I cleaned up the blood and got in the shower. I like to take showers in water so hot that for as brown as I am, I come out red. So, it was so steamy in the bathroom that it was getting hard to breath and just when I was about to get out I heard someone cough. I paused. How long had she been in the bathroom? I turned off the water and opened the curtain. She was leaning on the door watching me. "What's wrong?" she said in a sharp manner that threw me off just a bit. "Nothing." I said looking confused. Her whole demeanor had changed in a manner of seconds, and returned to calm in a matter of a few more. A smile suddenly appeared on her face and she ran to me with a towel to dry me. For some strange reason I didn't want her anywhere near me. I let her dry me though and I went into the room to get dressed, and she was behind me every step of the way.

She told me not to take too long because breakfast was about done and she didn't want it to get cold. I put my sweats back on and stuff, minus the panties, and headed down the stairs. The layout she had for breakfast was wonderful. Once I saw it I wanted to eat it, so I did. I was very good. It was about eleven o'clock in the morning, which is just as bad as eight o'clock to me because I don't really like to get up before twelve thirty, one o'clock. I felt good though because I was full and well rested. I slept the sleep of the dead last night. When I had cum, I let lose a lot of pent up energy and frustration. It felt nice. My body slept with less weight on it, it seems and I just wanted to be a bum today. I really didn't say much at breakfast and I didn't know where to begin. I wanted to forget all about it but I knew that was easier said than done. After I was done, I cleaned my plate and cleared the table. I told her breakfast was great and she wanted to see me later but I told her I was going to get up with Weezy and see what she was doing first. "Oh well, when you're done with her, you can come back and I'll take you out to a nice restaurant and when we get back, I'll run you a bath." She quickly said. As nice as that sounded, I really wasn't too interested in seeing her any time soon, so I said I'd call her and let her know. While I was getting dressed I called the car service, and told them to come in forty five minutes, and when my phone rang it was perfect timing. I had to get the hell out of there. I gave her a hug, told her thank you for a wonderful evening, and headed for the door. She just stood there looking confused. Like she really didn't understand that I had to go. On the way home, or on the way back to the hotel, I was thinking so hard that I had a headache. By the time I got upstairs to the hotel room I thought my nose was going to bleed. I took some Tylenol as soon as I stepped in the room. Weezy yelled for me and when I didn't come, she came into the bathroom. I was sitting on the toilet with my face in my hands.

"Girl, what's wrong?" She wanted to know. Weezy was still in her pajamas.

"I have a headache." I said with my face still in my hands. I got up and walked past her back into the bedroom. Being in some pajamas didn't sound like a bad idea right about now. I just wanted to get in my bed and be alone. I couldn't even begin to gather my thoughts correctly enough to explain to her what had happened the night before. Weezy rambled on about some different things that had occurred between her and Mr. Ring-a-ding and the different places she went and the different things they did. I didn't hear a word that was coming out of her mouth. I put Floetry in the CD player, put the music on low, and acquired the remote to the flat screen. I got under the covers and looked at the menu for room service. Weezy came over and sat on the bed.

"So what happened at Whyheeda's?" Weezy requested to know. I didn't even get to crack my lips when there was a knock at the door. Weezy got up and answered it. "Hey girl, good to see you! What are you doing here? We were just talking about you!" I heard Weezy say moments after she opened the door. What the hell was she doing here? I just fucking left her house. Weezy, not knowing the situation, ushered her into my room and they both sat on the bed. "What's going on girl?" Weezy said all cheery. "Nothing much, I just thought I might hang out with the two of you today." I looked at her like she was crazy but Weezy didn't catch it. "We didn't have anything in particular to do today, why? What did you have in mind?" Weezy said eagerly. I wanted Weezy to turn her head so she could see my face but her back was to me, because she was sitting on the side of the bed closest to where I was laying. Why talked about the same idea she fed to me before I left about the restaurant thing and then going back to her place for some drinks or something. I told them that they could go ahead 'cause I really wasn't in the mood to do anything but stay right where my body was planted. I picked up the phone while the two of them talked. I ordered some hot wings, a tuna salad, and a pot of hot apple tea. Whyheeda gave me a very displeasing look. Weezy left the room because her phone rang.

It was her Mr. Dick. I could tell by the special ring she gave him. I just watched the cartoons that were on, trying not to say a word.

"If you wanted some more to eat all you had to do was say something." Why said, with a slight sound of hurt in her voice and a slight hint of anger on her face.

"I was full when I left and I wanted something more heavy. Breakfast was great. I loved it." She just gave me a blank look. "What are you doing here?" I continued. "I told you I'd call you."

"Did you tell Louise about last night, about us?" What the hell was she talking about "us"? What the hell was this "us" shit?

"No I didn't tell her, and what do you mean by "us?" Look Whyheeda, I enjoyed your company. You were the best thing to happen to me since Blair died. What you gave me I will cherish always, and I will never forget you. You are the most beautiful woman I've ever seen, inside and out. Last night was something I can't even begin to explain, but that's just it. It was last night and that's all. While I don't want to change what has occurred between us, I can't help but to wonder if it was a mistake. I had a moment of great weakness and it broke me, but you helped put me back together. I was in shock when I woke up this morning and I didn't know how to handle it. I'm sorry, that was not the best display of myself earlier. I apologize." I was glad I got that off my chest. She just sat there and then she started crying. I felt terrible. I reached out to hug her and she slapped me! What the fuck was that!?

"You think you can just play with people's emotions like that?" She said crying, then she just got up. The only thing that kept me from choking her to death was the simple fact that Weezy didn't need to be caught in no drama, I know she was mad, and her feelings were hurt. I didn't respond. "You think you can just sleep with me and throw me to the dogs?" Weezy would happen to walk in the room when Whyheeda said that shit. "You're not going to get rid of me that easy!" She said, and then Whyheeda stormed past Weezy crying and out the front door.

"What the hell is she talking about?" Weezy said. She was all confused! Weezy looked like she was about to run after her for slamming the door. Weezy hated when people did that. I told Weezy to sit down and I told her everything. I told her how I had been feeling and all the things running through my mind. I told her everything word for word that was said that night and everything that happened from the time I walked in the door till the time I walked out. Weezy just sat there with a look of pure and utter shock on her face by the time I was done. She didn't say a word for quite some time and finally I had to say something.

"Well? What are you thinking?" I said. She continued to remain in the shock I found her in when the story I was telling began. She started to stutter.

"I, I, ...don't know what to say!" She finally blurted out. "Why in the hell didn't you tell me?" She screamed and blurted out once more.

"I don't know! How in the hell was I supposed to tell you I was daydreaming about fucking a woman that I've just barely known for twenty four hours?"

"Oh, I don't know Simone! You could have started with, "Weezy, I'm thinking about fucking a woman I met just over twenty four hours ago!" She screamed. "Simone, I'm your best friend, if not family, sisters even! You could have talked to me about what was going through your mind girl. Remember that time you told me you and Blair double-teamed some woman 'cause the two of you thought she was pretty? Bitch please." She rolled her eyes.

I just sat and listened. She always had a way of making me feel better with little crass comments. This bitch is just down right funny. I continued to give her the details and answered any questions she had about the whole ordeal, especially the sex. She said, 'if the sex was no good then it was a waste of time'. I liked Whyheeda a lot and I felt so bad about what I did to her. I didn't mean to hurt her. I was just weak and I had needs that needed to be met and that's what happened. I don't want to be with her though. She made things just a little too weird too quickly. After Weezy and I discussed that matter a little while longer, I decided to lay down and take a nap. We were leaving in the morning and I had to wash clothes and pack. I had been sleeping for maybe an hour when I was awakened by my cell phone ringing. I was reluctant to answer it, due to the fact that I was having a most wonderful sleep, but it was the fifth time that it had rang. I rolled over to see who was blowing up my phone, and it was Whyheeda. It was she who had called all the other times before. I turned the ringer off and went back to sleep. I woke up around six thirty that night and started packing and getting my things together to go. All the while thinking about my trip and how I was ready to go home. Despite the recent events that had occurred, I was quite happy. Weezy was right, I did need this vacation. I had money and a good friend, plenty of family, I was set. I missed Blair so much still, but it didn't hurt as bad anymore. Not only was my mind letting him go but so was my body. I was completely done and ready to go by ten o'clock. I took a shower because from running all around the room I had built up a little sweat and I would rather be shot before I get in my bed like that unless it starts there, if you know what I mean. In the midst of me running the water for the shower, I decided to take a bath. So, I plugged up the tub, poured in the oil and the soap, and let it fill. I got undressed and submerged my body in the steaming hot water. Blair never liked taking baths with me because he said I always made the water too hot. He would get in the shower though. I lay back and enjoyed the sounds of my own heartbeat and I'm elated by the feeling of being alive.

 The next day Weezy and I are sitting in the airport waiting to board our plane. We got there two hours early as instructed and had a few minutes to burn, so we gathered our carry-on bags and took a walk to the ice cream store. We, for some reason, didn't say much. It was already assumed, what was assumed, I don't know, but we understood it either way.

"We had a good time didn't we?" I said breaking the silence between us, but not the noise in the airport.

"We sure did!" Weezy said with a quiet look. "I think I'm in love." She blurted out.

"What! In love? With who? When, why, and how?" I said almost choking on the rum raisin. Weezy just laughed. "Damn girl, Mr. Morris put it on you huh!" Now I was cracking up.

"Girl, I don't know what happened, but something about him makes me smile, and it's not just the sex either!" She said, "Ronald and I were in love when we were in college, but our schedules wouldn't allow for it. I loved him then and I thought I was over him but, he has really changed since college and in all the right ways. When I kissed him for the first time it was like we were back on campus making out on a blanket on the yard." Weezy looked off into the distance as if she could see the picture she so vividly painted.

"Wow Weez!" "I had no idea." We paused for a moment and tasted our ice cream.

"How come you never told me about him?" I questioned.

"Well, it was a part of my past that I had left behind and like magic, it reappeared."

I smiled and felt happy for my best friend. I know it has been a while since she's felt this way about another man. I don't know what he did to her, but I'm glad he did it. Weezy and I got on the plane and headed back to our lives as we last knew it before we left. All the while knowing that the wind of change was blowing in our direction. After flying Weezy and I were tired from the trip but was more than happy to see a nice chilled bottle of Gran Spumante in the back of the limo assigned to pick us up from the airport. We sipped and relaxed as we left the airport. If it wasn't for the fact that we were so beat we would have done some shopping in the airport. Atlanta's airport is like an overpriced mall. It's so big. I've always loved airports, ever since I was a little kid. The ginger bubbles of the sparkling wine relaxed me on the drive home. Weezy and I still not talking much, just basked in the lights that seemed to shine new. The world looks different when you have a few bucks. I looked over at Weezy and thanked God for her, for she truly was the definition of a friend. We had really been through a lot together. I loved the fact that I could tell her any and every little thing on my mind and not be judged for it. The lights passed over the sun roof of the car and I was in a trance. I just sat back and let the bubbly and lights take me. As I wheeled my luggage to my door I couldn't help but feel, I don't know, strange. Like something wasn't quite right. I just turned the key and went in. The next day I called the job and let them know I was home and that everything was okay. I still had three days before I had to be back and I could use the rest. Weezy and I had drank, and I smoked so much I couldn't tell up from down. I had a really good time. Later on that night Weezy came down at like ten thirty at night, telling me all about her conversation with her new love. Weezy and I of course were night owls, so this wasn't odd. Besides, she had a key anyway. It wasn't uncommon for me to come out my bedroom and find her in my kitchen eating cereal and reading my paper. "Must you walk around ass naked?", she'd ask, and I'd tell her, "Must you eat the last of the Captain Crunch?" I hadn't seen her glow like this in a long time and it made me feel good that she was happy. I pulled out some Ben & Jerry's Chunky Monkey from the freezer and we stayed up talking until two in the morning. I told her that in depth details about Whyheeda and I told her about the sex and everything. I kinda told her about it when we were back in New Orleans, right before we left, but I didn't give her the meat and potatoes until then. She sat and watched me tell the story like she was watching a movie. All curled up with her legs crossed, at the foot of the couch bed. Every now and again we would sleep out there. I never used to sleep on it until after Blair, well, you know. We just always love returning to our bed. There was nothing like our bed. The most wonderful things happened behind that door when the lights went out. I still have light scratch scars on both sides of my stomach because one night he came so hard that he balled my flesh up into his hands. I didn't even notice until I went to go to the bathroom later on in the middle of the night and there was blood smeared all over me. My skin was torn a little just above my hips on each side. It looked like I had survived a wild cat attack. I was bruised and there was dry blood all over me. I called him from the bathroom, "Blaaair!?", and before I could get his name out a second time he came running in the bathroom. He freaked out. There was blood on him too. We went to the ER and everything. He apologized for that every time he looked at them and he would kiss the wounds. Now they are just eight light scratches. To me they looked like Tiger stripes. Weezy and I laughed about this as well. I woke up in the morning to find that Weezy had gone and so was my Chunky Monkey. For the rest of my vacation I cleaned house, cleaned car, went food shopping, caught up on phone calls, sent gifts home to my momma and daddy from the trip, and bought some new clothes. I couldn't help but feel though, that still, something wasn't right. I had been home for about three weeks and I was in the gym working out downstairs on the late night like I love to do. I sat in the sauna and relaxed. I liked to think about Blair in here. It was quiet and allowed me to concentrate on my thoughts. It was as if I could see them in my head clear as day. Weezy couldn't join me today 'cause Ronald had flown in for the week to see her. He would have dinner and everything waiting for her when she came in from work, and he treated her like a queen. She deserved it. I'd had all the happy I was supposed to have I guess. It was someone else's turn. That's how I tried to see things. I hadn't seen Weezy almost the whole time he was here. We all went bowling one night and had a blast. He's very charming, and a gentleman to the fullest. I liked him, mostly 'cause he made my best friend in the whole wide world laugh in the way a best friend couldn't. Other than that though, I hadn't really seen her. He was leaving in a day or two. The sauna was wonderfully still. There was a built- in CD player in the wall outside in a room next to the sauna so

THE NEXT BEST THING

you could play music. I brought my good friend Cassandra Wilson down and let her ride my imagination. All was quiet and all was right with the world until, baaaaaaaammmmm!!! A loud noise jolted me up off the bench where I had been laying. I carefully walked to the window. I didn't see anyone and I didn't hear anything, to which I noticed the music had stopped. All I could think in my head was, "I am not going to die in the gym of my own building like the white girls in the movies!" When I felt the time was right, I hauled ass outta that damn gym as fast as my legs could take me, titties flying and all. I put my shirt on, on the way out the door. I ran over to the security guard at the front desk and told him what I had heard. I explained to Albert what I was doing and what happened. Albert told me to calm down and he went into the locker room. I followed close behind him much to his protest, but I went anyway. My wallet and shit was in there! I wasn't going to just forget about it. If there was someone in there trying to steal, I would have beat them like they owed me money. Albert said that he didn't see anyone come in and he'd been sitting there for a while. His last bathroom break was three hours ago. We went into the little room next to the sauna 'cause that's where the noise came from, only to find that the sound system had been smashed out the wall. "Something real big must have hit it." Albert said with a confused look, and then turned to look at me. I told him not to even think what I think he was thinking. "Al, come on now. You know I come down to work out and chill, that's it. I don't bust shit up for no damn reason, and you know how I feel about my CD's!" I went to my locker and the lock had been taken off. All of my belongings were all over the floor, which wasn't much, a wallet, my sneakers and some CD's I keep down here to change the music in the system. I had this locker for God knows how long. My wallet had been emptied all over the bench, but nothing was missing. All my plastic and paper was still there, and that's all I cared about for the moment. I gathered my things together and after talking with the police and receiving an escort, I went back to my apartment. I locked the door behind me and felt better that I was in the comfort of my home once more. I called Weezy to tell her what happened, but she didn't answer the phone. I need to calm down, so I took a nice hot shower and applied some Bath and Body Works, Sandalwood Smoothing oil, and put on some pj's. I called Weezy a few more times but she just wasn't letting anything spoil her fun. I was tired and after watching some SpongeBob, I went to sleep. I drank a lot of water before I went to bed last night 'cause of all the working out. Most of the time I don't even get up in the middle of the night, but I went to pee. I went into the bathroom and turned on the light. I tried once, going without the light on and we'll not mention the rest. It was quiet and I had a long day in the morning. My sub-fuel compound was up for review and it was looking pretty good, but there was still some testing to be done. I turned out the light and everything was now pitch black 'cause I jacked up my night vision with those one hundred watt bulbs in the bathroom. I could have found my bed with my eyes closed though. Next thing I know I heard something shuffle and I laid down and went to sleep, but I wasn't in my bed and had a splitting headache. I awoke the next morning feeling well rested and dazed. When I tried to pick myself up, I just fell back down. My head was killing me and the smell of a familiar scent, one I know all too well, was lingering in the room. Everything in the room seemed to be moving even though I was laying still. I was scared. I didn't know what was happening, not to mention I had a board meeting with my superiors and their bosses about what they had been funding. I thought, how in the hell was I going to work if I couldn't get off the floor. I was rolling in one direction and the room seemed to be going in the other, so I vomited and passed out. When I awoke once more I could tell it was like late in the morning. I tried to get up and head to a phone because I now smell the blood and vomit that was resting only hairs from me. I tried to move but quickly realized my hands and feet were bound and just rolled over to my side. I tried to remember what happened but the headache I had would not let me put the pieces back together. I was still dizzy, but not quite like before. Then, came a voice. "It'll wear off in a little bit, don't worry." And until then I had completely forgotten the fact that I didn't do this to myself and that someone was in the apartment. The gym, coming out of the bathroom, all of it started running together, and then the smell. I keep a bottle of Blair's colon because sometimes I would wear it, but just around the house, or I would spray it in my bed after I put on some fresh sheets. This scent was heavy in the room like someone was wearing it and I knew it wasn't me, and that's when it hit me, Whyheeda! What the fuck! Please do not tell me this bitch broke into my apartment and got me tied up on the damn floor!! This shit was not happening. "Whyheeda, what are you doing?" I said with disappointment. I couldn't see her. She was sitting in a chair in the room behind me. I dare not even turn around. "Hi baby!" She said in a playful voice. "I told you that you would see me again!" She walked over to me and grabbed my shoulder and wrenched me onto my back. "OOOOhhhh, you stink!" She said. Now even though I was tied up, I could believe she just told me I stink. I pride myself on the way I smell and pay good money for the scents that adorn my body. I didn't care what was going on, I had to tell her about that shit.

"I slept in a pool of my own vomit and blood all night, what the fuck do you expect me to smell like?" I was pissed. "We're going to have to run you a bath!" She said happily, like what she was doing was in no way fucked up. I couldn't believe this shit was happening. While she was in the bathroom I tried to get my hands free, but I couldn't. I rolled over and got up on my knees. I leaned back to put the weight on my feet, but as soon as I stood up everything started moving and my nose started bleeding. What the hell was wrong with me. "Sit still!" Whyheeda ordered as I was knocked back down to the floor with a hard object. I could feel that the flesh on the side of my face was open. The warm blood trickled down like beads of sweat after basketball. "What did you give me?" I asked, trying not to throw up again. "Oh, not much.

Just a little heroin." She laughed. "I could tell you've never done drugs. You don't seem to be taking it too well." "I thought I overdosed you at one point because you started convulsing and sweating. I didn't think you were going to make it." All this she said with a smile. She grabbed me by the ankles and dragged me into the bathroom. She took some scissors and cut off the little clothing I had on and heaved me in the tub. I couldn't even sit myself up. Heroin! Did this bitch say she gave me heroin? Oh hell no! If I could lift my chin right now I'd head butt the shit out of her. Heroin!

"Heroin though?" I asked. "So this is what it feels like to be high! This shit fucking sucks!!" "Who in the hell does this for fun?" I was in the tub, but I couldn't feel the water. I could tell it was hot though because just having my face so close to it was making it hard to breathe. I knew I was going to feel this bath eventually. "Are you comfy?" I just looked at her with the one eye I could open when she said that. "Hell no I'm not fucking comfy. What the fuck are you doing here? How did you get into my house? Do you think you're gonna get away with this? If I wasn't all fucked up I….." I didn't get to finish that last sentence because she grabbed me by the throat and under the water I went. I tossed and turned. I couldn't put up much of a fight and I was so weak from the drugs. The blows to my damn skull didn't help much either. The hot water was burning my face and the cuts. Everything started to get real quiet like. I could hear my heart beating slower and slower. Is this the way I was going to die? I felt sleepy. I thought it was the end. Then, as I was watching my life flash before my eyes, she pulled me up. I coughed and choked. "Now are we ready to be quiet?" She said, still smiling. "What do you want? Why are you here? Why are you doing this?" I managed to cough out. "I told you, you were not going to just love me and leave me. I'm sick of people doing that to me. Sleeping in my bed, and then just discarding me, no! It's not going to happen that way!" She continued to talk and somehow I managed to get my hands free. I was waiting for just the right time to cold cock her in the jaw and haul ass. She washed me as she spoke. Paying close attention to my breasts, as if to admire them. Whyheeda was crazy. I think they let her go from that hospital for a whole lot more than what she had told me at dinner at her house. The heroin was still on me heavy, but I was not as confused as before. Both my hands were now free. I didn't know how I did it, 'cause it took everything in me. I think she intended to kill me with the drugs, but she didn't give me enough. She gave me a lot, but I guess not enough to kill me. I pretended that the drugs had taken over and played dumb for a minute. "You look so beautiful, now that we got all that shit off your face. I'm going to have you one last time before I kill you." Whyheeda said, but this time she wasn't smiling. That was my queue to get the hell out of dodge. She leaned in to kiss me and that's when I took my chance. I balled my fist up and with every bit of strength I had left in me, I popped the hell outta of her ass. She fell back and hit her head on the edge of the sink and hit the floor. I fell over her trying to get past her but I made it. I was stumbling to the door butt naked and dripping wet. I was home free until…BANG! I was so stoned that I did know what had happened until I noticed I was no longer walking to the door. I also was no longer standing up. I could feel a warm liquid escaping from my back, and when I rolled over on my side there was a gaping hole opposite that wet feeling. I've been shot. I tried to crawl toward the door, but I was dragged back into the bedroom. I could see the trail of blood I was leaving as I went. She wrapped me in a towel and hoisted me up on the bed. Not before giving me a good stiff kick to the ribs. The shot hurt so bad I didn't feel it anymore. After laying me on the bed she beat me with the butt of the pistol until my eyes were shut permanently. I could hear her crying. She lay on the bed next to me. "All I ever wanted to do was love you. I could have made you happy." She cried over me. It was hard for me to breathe now and instead of vomit, this time my mouth was filled with blood. I lay there thinking of Blair. I started to think back to that first night that we fucked, had sex, and made love all in one night. Yes, there is a difference for those who don't know. I thought about how he would be so gentle with me, and then at times rip me in two. My eyes were swollen shut, but I could see him in my head as clear as daylight through my window on Sunday mornings. Whyheeda continued to talk. I knew that this was the end for me. Weezy was upstairs with Ronald and she thought I was at work. That's why she didn't come down this morning. I wish I could have told Blair I loved him one more time. I wish I could have told Weezy how much she meant to me just once more. I wanted to call my mother and tell her thank you for not giving up on my life by getting rid of me. I wish I could wrap my arms around her one more time. If I could see my father again I'd tell him that I'll always be daddy's little girl, no matter how old I get. By now Whyheeda had gotten off the bed and stood in front of it. I hadn't really been paying attention to anything she had been saying. I knew I was inches from death. I wasn't cold or anything. I think I was in shock. I did however feel the syringe full of heroin she inserted in my leg before she got up. I guess she thought, 'Well, I'ma kill her, but she'll die painless and with whatever is left of her smile.' Whoa..., heroin works fast. As my chest got heavier and heavier I heard the door get kicked in and a loud bang. I also heard someone screaming, 'get down.' My left leg felt strange and then there were two more loud bangs, and a bunch of footsteps. I heard people running all through the room and I couldn't hold on any longer. Between the rapid blood loss, drugs, and severe head trauma I didn't know up from down. I heard a voice in my ear. "Stay with Mone, stay with me! Bitch don't you leave me. We've been through too much. Come on!!!" First dead silence and then came sleep.

It was really quiet. I could hear people talking, it seemed, not far from where I lay. I could hear the wind blowing in through the window, and the breeze on my face felt good. I could hear clicks and beeps, and a machine that exhaled when I did. I was alive. I was damn alive. I made it. I tried to move, but I was stiff as a board. My whole face was throbbing. My left leg was raised up on a pillow with a bandage at the thigh. The sunlight was killing my eyes and I felt like ten pounds of shit in a five pound bag. A nurse came marching in the room with her clipboard and pens. "Well, look who's up! I'm your nurse Miss Allen." She said with a big smile on her face. I attempted to smile back, which made her smile more. "I've been looking after you since you've been here. You gave everyone a scare, but your heart was strong and you didn't give up." Miss Allen said. I looked around the room and there were so many flowers I felt like I was in Jumanji. I tried to talk but my throat was so dry so I reached for the water that was in the pitcher by the bed. Miss Allen noticed this occurring and quickly ran over to assist me. I don't know how far I was going to get with that water to my face, but I was going to try. I was having trouble just trying to lift my eyelashes, let alone lift my arms. Once I had some water in my mouth and on my lips I felt a little better. After some coughing, I managed to get out, "How long have I been out?" Miss Allen picked up my chart and looked it over for a few minutes. "You came in on the seventh,... and you just awakened from a ten day coma." What the fuck did she just say! A coma! Boy I tell you, just when you start to think you are invincible, something happens to remind you quickly. I started sweating and my mouth got dry again. I think I was panicking. All I could think of is that people die in comas. I wanted to get up and move real bad after that, so I tried to sit up but I couldn't. I found the button on the remote on the bed that sat it up. "Now don't you do no fussin'! You are alright now. You done made it through, but you gotta take it easy for a little while until you get your strength back. And don't you worry, it'll come quick if you work at it." Her words just reminded me of my grandmother. I just began to cry. I hadn't had a good cry in a long, long time. Miss Allen sat down on the bed next to me and pulled me to her. She rocked me and hummed a tune I know she made up in her head, but it didn't matter to me none. "There, there. Let it out. You're gonna be alright. God doesn't like it when someone tries to hurt his own. That girl that did what she did is going to receive her judgment."

And with Miss Allen's last words, the tears began to fade away. After giving me a check-up, Miss Allen left the room. She told me she'd be back soon with something for me to try to nibble on. Come to think about it, I was hungry. Another nurse came in not long after and took me to a bath full of hot water. I was undressed and put in the tub. As soon as I sat down in the water I had an instant flashback about what had just happened to me almost two weeks ago. I remember the almost scalding hot water I was almost drowned in. I remembered the burning sensation on my face and in my mouth. The same feeling of helplessness ran over me 'cause like then, I couldn't move. I saw her face in my mind playing over and over again like a skipping DVD. I just wanted it to stop. Something that once brought me so much joy and pleasure now made me uneasy and afraid. There were many nights Blair and I enjoyed ginger scented bubbles floating on hot water that adhered to our wet flesh, and us adhered to each other. It was clear now that it would be a long time before I took a bath again, or if I would ever take a bath again for that matter. Back in the room some time later, after I had been fed and dressed, I just sat on the bed watching my favorite cartoons. It was about eight o'clock and it finally dawned on me that I needed to let everyone know I was awake, but I didn't know if I was ready for the questions that were sure to swamp me once the ringing stopped for whoever answered on the other end. "Heeeeyyyy you!" Weezy came running in with some flowers. "They told me you were up and that I should give them some time to get you together before I came by." I could see the tears welding up in her eyes as she spoke. "Are you cold, are you hungry, thirsty, what, what do you need?" She was talking a mile a minute. "Weezy, I'm fine. I'm just a little worn down that's all." "Do you remember what happen at all?" She asked as if to shield me from the reality of it all. "Yeah, but I don't know what happened to my leg. The doctor is coming to talk to me tomorrow and explain everything that happened in detail." I understood what he was saying and all but, I wasn't up to listening to all that technical stuff at that point in time. Dr. Marone told me about the drugs and things I was given. Turns out that the heroin was mixed with a tranquilizer. He basically said she was trying to stop my heart but it was strong. Weezy sat on the bed and gave me the total story about what happened when she and the cops came in. That was the only thing that was kind of hazy. She told me that Whyheeda, in aiming for my chest, missed because she was startled by the cops kicking in the door and shot me in the leg. "She really was going to kill you. The drugs didn't do it to you so she was going to dope you up some more and shoot you when you passed out so you wouldn't feel it." I looked at Weezy all types of crazy when she said that. "I know, I know. Don't ask me what the hell she was thinking!" Weezy said, nodding her head back and forth with her hands in the air. Weezy said that she wasn't dead either. She was locked up in prison. Whyheeda had been shot twice in her left shoulder and was in recovery in prison. As soon as I get better we have to appear in court. My head began to hurt. I had my work cut out for me. I had to get back in shape and get myself together, and deal with this court trial. Just when I thought I was going to lose it, I looked up to the clouds and thanked God for being, before I was about to go through it. I could have been six feet under, but the almighty had other plans for me, ….. so I won't complain. Suddenly all I wanted to do was sing, "I've had some good days,." I used to sing "I Won't Complain" any time I had a large obstacle ahead that was promising to be an arduous one. Weezy just stopped talking and listened. We both knew that what was coming wasn't going to be pretty, but I was ready to deal with it and so was my best friend.

Eighteen months later, one trial, and a lot of therapy, things finally seemed to be back to normal. The trail was on the news and everything. I couldn't go anywhere for a while without a camera following me, or a reporter wanting to ask me a million questions. I got calls from every talk show in the country and had an article in Essence magazine titled, "When Crossing Over Crosses The Line." I had women hitting on me at every turn. One woman walked up on me in the supermarket and said, "I would never hurt you like that. I would treat you like the queen you are." I just wanted to scream on her right there in the dairy section, but I didn't. I could tell she genuinely felt bad for what happened to me. I smiled and thanked her and went on about my way. I was famous. For the longest time Albert would call me twice a day to come down and get some flowers left at the desk for me. He would call twice because I would take up the first shipment and then come back down for the rest that came during the day. Work was crazy. I got the grant for the continuation of the testing for my compound and soon it would be up for real world testing in one of the test jets. I was happy about that. I was also given a research team of my own to head, and my own lab. It just goes to show you, you can't have the good without the bad and vice versa. Everyone at the job was very supportive. When I had to run for therapy, some of them would come out and run in the park with me and the therapist. They didn't talk about what had happened. They were just glad I was okay and that I was back to work 'cause let's face it, I was a valuable asset to the company. If I left, so did my research. One day I had come in from the office as usual. It was a regular day, or as regular as it could be after what happened, and there was a letter from Oakdale Federal Correctional Facility. It was from Whyheeda, and I didn't want to open it at first. It sat on the coffee table all night. Weezy came down that night for some ice cream. She won't buy the stuff herself but she'll eat mine the hell up! She says, 'if she eats half, it'll save me from having all the fat.' I told her about the letter and as soon as she knew where it was she ran for it. She knew I wanted her to open it and she didn't hesitate either. "You want me to read it to you Mone?" she said as she unfold the paper. Before I could give an answer she started.

> Dear Simone,
>
> I know there is nothing that I can say that can make up for all the pain and heartache I've caused you. I

can only hope you find it in my heart to forgive me. I just lost my mind. My husband left me like so many men before him. I had been alone for a long time and you were the first person I had a connection with since my husband left me. They had been with me, but like you they split with the rising of the sun. I know this still doesn't excuse my behavior. ("You damn right it don't!!" Weezy said, like she was sitting there to hear her.) I just got tired of being alone and feeling used. I know now that was not your intention to make me feel that way. I know you asked nothing of me and made no promises but I saw what I wanted to see. I pray everyday for forgiveness and hope that you can find it in your heart to understand the sick and weary. You have to understand that I never wanted to end up this way, but you never know where life is going to take you. As you know I've been sentenced to die by lethal injection. I know this is a lot to ask, but I was wondering if I could see you one last time face to face. I just would like the opportunity to tell you to your face how sorry I am and beg for your forgiveness before I die. I had no right to try to take your life. There was someone out there who wanted you to live which is why luckily my twisted plans failed. There is no one coming to save me though. There is no one to save me from the fate I have sealed for myself. No one cares for me. You are lucky to have Louise. I envy what the two of you have and the love that you have for each other. I envy the love you shared with Blair. I wish my husband and I had had that kind of love. I'm sorry he was taken from you. Things happen for a reason though. If you could make it down here it would mean the world to me. Please forgive me.

Why.

Weezy just looked at me. I had left the kitchen and was now sitting on the love seat. "Are you going to go?" Weezy asked with great disbelief. "I..I, I don't know!" Was I going to go? For a while Weezy and I went over the pros and cons of this venture. There were a lot of good and a lot of bad. We also joked about some of the stuff that had happened. I could laugh about it now, but when that shit happened it was nowhere near close to funny. Weezy would ask me sometimes what it was like to be a dope head for a day. I know for a while my doctor was having me come in to see him once a week, just to see if I had started using it. Dr. Marone said it starts that way sometimes. Like, people try it and get hooked on the first take. It was funny. At first I was mad about the whole thing. I knew that wouldn't happen to me, but then again so did everyone else before they were on street corners beggin' to wash windows and much worse to get a hit. However, I got money so I would have just killed myself with what I would have been able to buy. "Simone, you don't owe her anything! She can rot in there for all I care, and you know what else?" I just turned to look at her. "I think she's getting off too easy by being put to death! She should spend the rest of her life in jail in a six by three foot room and only fed what was needed to keep her alive." I looked at her like, wow! "I'm serious Simone. I thought we I was going to lose you. You have been my family for a long time, my sister. She tried to take something from me that was dear, and to me that's like stealing and you know how I feel about a thief." I nodded in slight agreement and continued to eat my ice cream. "The big question here is not are you going to go, but do you want to go?" I looked at her and the look on my face must have given her an answer I didn't even know yet, 'cause she just took a deep breath. "Well, if you want me to go with you, just let me know." "I didn't say I was going." I laughed. "You don't have to say it. Just let me know when you want to go so I don't make any appoints." Weezy said going out the door. She was expecting a late night phone call from Ron. She told me that the two of them have phone sex when they are

THE NEXT BEST THING

not together. The two of them are in love something terrible and it's great. He also talking about moving up here to stay with her, but we'll see. Sometimes I sit around looking at my apartment and think about all the good memories I've had here. I wonder sometimes if I should leave. I wanted to buy a house but, it's just me and this apartment is great. I don't need a bigger space to be alone in, or do I? Weezy's life is coming together. I see her and Ron in this for the long run. I know Weezy's into the whole house thing 'cause she can't wait to settle down and have some kids. She always wanted to know when Blair and I was going to have some kids. She always said, 'as much as ya'll have sex! I don't see how you manage not to have none this long!' Blair and I wanted kids, but we just wanted to wait 'till we were married and I was done with the project. After the project, I would take some time off so we could make a baby. I know it wouldn't have taken us long. It seemed like things in my life were back in order but I needed to find peace of mind. My thoughts were scrambled a lot, and found that when I'm not at work, I really don't have the urge to do much. I have no zest for life. I'm going to go. I'm going to see her.

A few days later on my way in from work, I got a letter. I was from Blair's family. I halted in my footsteps then ran upstairs to rip the letter open. It was from his Aunt Martha, who lived in Green Island, Jamaica. Blair's mother was dying and requested for me to come to her bedside. I didn't know what to say. I hadn't really talked to his mother much after he passed. She knew I took it kind of hard and she understood. I didn't waste any time. It was eight thirty at night and I was trying to make plans to be on my way that evening, but I couldn't just leave like that. Not without saying something to Weezy and my parents. I called everyone on my staff that night and gave them a list of instructions to follow due to my absence. After I took care of work I blew up Weezy's cell. She was nowhere to be found. I went upstairs in her apartment and left her a letter telling her what was to happen. My plane was leaving first thing in the morning, and I had some laundry and packing to do. It was going to be a long night, but I didn't plan on sleeping anyway.

After everything was packed up and I had made all the phone calls I needed to make and left all the information I needed to leave, it was about three forty five in the morning. My plane was set to leave at ten, and Weezy still didn't call me back. "I wonder where the hell she's at?" Oh well! Weezy knew what to do when I was away on trips. My apartment was in good hands. She would babysit the place when I went to seminars and lectures. Blair would go with me just 'cause he could, and so neither one of us would be lonely. I loved him so. I often think about being with other men, but how? How do you go from having the best, to the next best thing? How do you go from having the world to owning a rock?

Six hours and a nap later, I'm on my way to Jamaica. I pulled out my laptop to do some work but didn't get too far. I was so sleepy I just nodded off and next thing I know I was in Jamaica. I felt like I was home. I didn't bring much with me. I didn't know how long I would be staying. If I needed anything, I'd just buy it when I got there. As soon as I got off the plane my phone was buzzing. I decided to wait 'till I got settled before I started with the one hundred and one questions. As I come out through customs, I see a sign with my name on it. He was a tall brown man with long locks that were very well kept. When the man noticed I was staring at him he started smiling and walked toward me. I began to walk toward him as well and I could see his brighter than white smile and perfectly aligned teeth. He had on an orange mesh tank top, that did nothing but compliment his complexion, and a pair of light brown, cargo wide legged shorts. The large holes in the shirt revealed a more than well built body kissed by the sun all over. His dreads poured over his shoulder like a mane, and I began to wonder what jungle he was king of. The stranger, once he reached me, put down the sign and said my name. "Simon?" His deep voice rang in my body like the gong of a large golden bell in a temple of great importance. "Yes." I answered, not only to answer his question, but also to hear him speak once more. "Hello! I'm pleased to meet you. My name is Armond, Armond Morgan. But, my friends call me Simba." He said with that wonderful smile. A breeze crept over his shoulder and down on me like an invisible wave of water. The smell of him instantly put me at ease. I thought to myself, 'What is that!' I love a smell that makes me turn my head, and this definitely qualifies as doing so. His huge frame shielded me from the sun shining in through the giant glass doors that appeared to be welcoming me to come through. "Nice to meet you Armond," and before I could finish he said, "Please! Call me Simba." "Okay, Simba. I'm Simone, Simone McKnight." "I've heard a lot about you from the family." He said, still with one of the most beautiful smiles I ever seen, on his face. "Come, I'm here to take you to my aunt's house. Out of everyone that wanted to be here with her, to care for her, she wanted you to do it! Do you know why?" I just shrugged my shoulders. By now we were walking toward the car. "Blair and I are cousins. We were close when we were little, but he went to America and I went to England, I guess we just grew apart. We still talked every once in a while though." It wasn't hard to tell that somewhere along the lines they had shared some of the same genes. Armond was beautiful, just like Blair. I watched the biceps in his arms tighten as he placed my bags in the truck of his Cadillac CTS-V, the car of my dreams. I don't know why I haven't bought one yet. I mean, it's not like I don't have the money. I'll think about selling my car when I go back home. Anyway, he was telling me about Blair as a kid and the different things they used to get into, and I just listened contently. Armond began to tell me about the family that I was going to meet when I got there, and about the property that the house was on. I was taken by the views already on the way there. I wasn't even worried about it being nice. The culture swept me off my feet alone, right along with this brown man sitting next to me smelling so good. I wasn't sure what was happening to me, but I just wanted to lick him. His voice started to fade out after a while. I just let the smell of him invade all my senses. The ride to the house was about four and a half hours long. So, needless to say, since I had been up all night and traveling all day, I was kind of tired. I lasted about a good three hours of the ride and then I was gone with wind. It was evening by the time we arrived, and I was awakened by a gentle caress to my check. A soft voice of a woman rang gently in my ear. I awoke to a whole bunch of people staring in the car. I sat up stunned and confused. The older woman who woke me opened the door, grabbed my hand, and with a firm but gentle grip, ushered me out of the car. I turned toward the trunk of the car to so I get my things out. Before I could even turn my body in the direction my head was facing the old woman said, "Your things were already taken care of." I had begun to wonder how long I had been sleeping in the car before they woke me? And furthermore, how long were they watching me sleep? That's how I know I was tired and stressed out 'cause Armond was moving in and out of the car to get my things out and I didn't wake or stir not once. Everyone was just staring at me. I hadn't thought about all the other people being there. At least I had spoken to his mother a few times, I mean, I didn't know any of these folks. Everywhere I turned there were dreads, beards, and thick accents. I didn't know what I was going to do. I was so nervous and the old woman could tell. Once she got me in the house, on the way up the stairs, she told me to, 'Ease your mind chil.' She asked me if I was hungry and thirsty. I wasn't at first but my nerves had changed all that. My mouth was dry as shit. I didn't say much of anything since I got out the car. We finally arrived at my room after what seemed like forever. We entered the room and turned on the lights. The room was beautiful. There were live spider plants hanging all over the room, and a large king size bed in the middle of the room that sat atop of three small steps. There was a canopy that was rolled up along the top side of the frame of the bed. It was really big and the air in the room smelled sweet. There was a balcony but it was too dark outside to see anything. The hardwood floor was newly polished and the bed freshly made. There were all kinds of plush pillows all over the bed too. The room was full of fall earth toned colors like different shades of light and dark browns, pea greens, soft oranges, and yellows. It was a large room. There was a small living room set up in front of the bed, so that I could either watch TV from bed or from the couch. There was a desk with a fully loaded computer, fax machine, and phone. Now I could check on things at work a lot more. The desk furniture was made of red oak, and you could smell the wood when you got close to it, like it was just cut and put together. The woman walked me over to the bed and sat me down. She just stared at me for a minute. She reached her hand out and caressed my cheek once more as if it would help her to see me better. "Welcome chil. Welcome to our home." Her voice was soft but deep. She told me that the woman I had come to see was resting and that I would see her as soon as she and I were both ready for our day tomorrow. She got up and pointed me to my private bathroom, which I overlooked in my amazement with the scenery. She told me she'd be back soon with something to eat and drink, despite my soft protest. I just sat there for a minute to soak it all in. I didn't know where the hell I was or how in hell to get back for that matter! I got up and walked in the bathroom that opened up into a whole notha' room. The shower was separate from the tub. There was a long vanity and on the other side there was another counter with two sinks. The bathroom was gorgeous. It was like something out of a five star resort. You had to walk through the closet area to get to the bathroom. The bathroom's theme was cream and red. Simply put, it was lovely. There were all kinds of oils and scents neatly set up on the vanity. I could tell that they were all new and had never been used. I wondered if they had put those there for me. "It couldn't be though! On such short notice?" I said to myself. But then again, they had sent me a letter knowing I would come. I don't know. I was still wound up from this whole thing and wanted to bring myself down, so I decided to take a nice hot shower. The water in the shower seemed to be like liquid silk touching me all over. I don't know what kind of soap I was using but it was nice. After the shower I was ready for bed. On my way to the bed, where my bags were so comfortably placed, the woman came back. "Oh, I see ya took a shower!" "Yes ma'am." I replied to her observation and continued along with dressing. The woman started setting up the little table with something on it that smelled absolutely delectable. My mouth began to water while I watched her. She stopped working when she noticed I was still sitting in my towel on the bed. "Go on, get dressed." She smiled, so I did. She came over to lotion my back for me, and I sat down to the adorable table she had set so quickly. She had brought some salmon and rice and vegetables, a bowl of all kinds of cut fruit and some sorrel to drink with little chunks of ice. I could tell that the ice had been broken off from a block. I thanked her, blessed the food, and stuffed my face. The first bite paused me in my tracks, as the taste of food not only dissolved on my palate, but it dissolved my discomfort for now. She just sat there in a rocking chair in the corner of the room, watching, making sure everything was to my liking, which it was. I ate like I had never had a meal before, but it seemed to please her that I found her dish to be so appetizing. As soon as I finished the last bit, as if on queue, the lady got up and started pulling down the rolled up curtains on the bed and opened the curtain that consisted of two halves to open and close as an exit on the side she wished me to enter the bed on. "Come!" She called to me, and I got up and walked over to her without hesitation or question. She pulled back the sheets as I walked up the royal-like steps. The woman stood until I was safely and comfortably nested in one spot. "Ma'am do you have a name?" I asked, because she had said something about everything I passed in the house and in the room, but she forgot herself. She smiled at me and adjusted my hair on my right shoulder. "Chil dem all call me Nana. I take care of tings round here." I loved her smile. Her teeth looked like old pearls, but they were still pearls nonetheless. They were a little worn, but they were as white as hope. "Rest and we'll catch you all up in de mornin'." She closed one side of the curtain and left a low light illuminating the room, and shut the door. I was very tired. This seemed like a dream, and I didn't want to wake up from this one either! I don't know? Maybe I should stop falling into dreams while I'm awake so I could have something to do when I'm sleep. I just lay there alone with my thoughts, which all seemed to be running together at this time. I was watching my day play out in my head, my own private TV. There were reruns of Armond, and I kept watching over and over again, until my TV went black.

I woke up the next morning to the smell of something good! I heard birds chirping and a breeze swaying. The curtain that was up when I fell asleep was now down. I knew it was day-break, but I didn't know the time. I didn't want to get out of the bed at all. I slept better last night than I had in a long time. The bed was soft and made to cater to my, and mine only, comfort needs. Or, well so it seemed. The next thing I know I hear a curtain being opened but it was not the ones around the bed. I was hungry now 'cause whatever, whoever was cooking, I now wanted some. I pulled back the curtain to peek my head out of the bed. There was no one there. The dishes from last night were taken and there were new dishes with more and different food, all set and ready for me to meet and greet. I found my house shoes next to the bed waiting for me as well. I got up and walked over to the tray. There was some fried pla-ton, eggs, bacon, some banana pancakes and a tall glass of orange juice. It was fresh from the stove 'cause I still see the heat escaping. I walked over to the balcony that had once caught my attention last night and opened the door. The sight that was before me almost brought a tear to my eyes. It was lovely. There were trees all over the place and a garden that was most heavenly. It had all kinds of flowers that were different shapes, sizes, and colors. The air was sweet to smell and to taste. It appeared that I was on some type of estate.

There were gardeners on lawn mowers and some with hoes. There were three horses being walked around by some dark chocolate men wearing large tan hats to keep the sun out their faces. The grass was soo thick it looked like carpet. It was really green. Almost like it was painted that color. The house was large also. There was a table and some chairs out on the balcony, so I decided to sit and eat my breakfast out there. I was turned on by the sheer magnificence of it all. I just wanted to run naked through the garden, and little did I know at that time that wish was soon to come true. After I was done eating I sat for a few moments to collect my thoughts. I didn't know what I was going to say to Miss Armstrong. I also had no idea what she was going to ask me, or why I, of all the people in the family had to be here. After another moment or two I got myself together. I cleaned up my dishes and my crumbs, and got dressed. I was carrying the tray with the dishes when I left out of the room so I could return the tray to the kitchen. I wasn't wearing anything special. I had on a red wife beater with a small Enyce logo in the front with some khaki cargo shorts, and khaki pumas. I don't really wear that much jewelry. I wore Blair's engagement ring for a while and then I took it off and put it into my storage vault in the bank. I couldn't bear the thought of it being stolen or if I lost it, which would never happen, but never say never. I do however wear a chain around my neck, a silver bracelet Blair bought me, with scorpions on it, and my class ring and watch. That's pretty much an everyday thing. I opened the door to the room and looked out into the hallway. The place looked much different during the day. There were hardwood floors all over the house. They were very well kept and the surface had a mirror finish. There was a whined staircase and a big alabaster statue in the middle of the foyer of a woman. It seemed to be as if no one was home. Either that, or they were all outside. I wondered how my people lived here, 'cause it seems to be like a lot of them from what I remember from last night. I stood in front of the statue looking into its face. For some strange reason I could have swore that statue looked like me. The woman was naked, but her hair covered between her legs, the crack of her buttocks, and her right breast. I could have sworn that statue was me! I know my hair isn't that long, but I've been living with my body long enough to know it if I were staring at it. "It's beautiful, isn't it?" The familiar voice of a man said. It was Armond. He looked even better today than he did yesterday. His dreads were pulled back, which exposed his strong neck and shoulders. He had on a white tank top and shorts set that matched perfectly with his smile. Looking at him just made you want to smile. "Good morning Armond." I said hesitantly. His deep voice startled me and I had to recover a little before I began to speak. "No, no! Call me Simba. You are my friend aren't you?" Armond said looking slightly offended, but not mad, and I smiled back. "Okay then. 'Cause I want to be friends with you." He smiled. He had no idea what that statement did to my clitoris. Armond, I mean SIMBA, had no idea how friendly I was in a mood to let him get. "Well SIMBA,..", I said back with a smile. He nodded his head with approval. "Where is everyone?" "Everyone's outside, we were waiting for you to get up 'cause we didn't want to wake you. You looked exhausted and stressed yesterday, so we decided to let you be until you felt like coming down." Wow, so they were waiting on me. I feel bad now for taking my time coming downstairs. Simba took the tray from me and told me that everyone was in the garden, which made me think. That garden must be bigger than I know, because I would have seen them from the view I had, and I didn't hear anyone. "I was on my way to check on you when I found you staring at your statue." He took a moment to admire it too. "What! This is a statue of me?" I knew I wasn't crazy. "Yeah, Blair had it made for you after he proposed and it was to be a gift to you." I looked at him like he was telling a lie that I knew was truth. If I would have been holding that tray boy, I think I would have dropped it. "Yup! Blair was planning on getting the two of you a house," Then he turned to look at the statue, "It was to go into the garden that he was going to build for you." Simba turned back to me. I didn't know what to say. I felt a little light headed and had to sit down, even if there wasn't a chair. Simba quickly put the tray on the floor and grabbed me. He walked me to a chair staged not far from us and sat me down. He told me he'd be right back, got the tray, and disappeared into the left hallway. The light pouring in from the ceiling high windows was starting to make my head spin. A house! He was buying us a house. He was going to build me a garden! I remember the day we first had the conversation about what our first house was going to be like. I remember it like it was yesterday. Blair and I had gone to this remote park that a friend of his had told him about. It was at least an hour away from the apartment. We packed a big lunch, brought a small tent, blanket and pillows, and a CD player. We found this great spot by a river at the end of a forest. We were tired as shit by the time we finally got to where we found a comfy spot from carrying all that stuff. It was so nice that day. We laid out in the shade talking about our future like, how many kids we wanted and when, and what our first house was going to be like. I remember telling him that I wanted a big garden in the back. I wanted the plants to stand tall enough so that you couldn't see straight through it. I want there to be a path made through it all, and open in the middle like a clearing in the center of a jungle. I wanted all kinds of flowers and things, and told Blair that when it was done, we would make love in the garden so it would grow with love. I put my hands to my face and began to cry after my trip down memory lane brought me back to reality. I got up and walked over to the statue and hugged it, and continued to cry. "Thank you baby." I said hoping Blair could hear me where he was. "It's beautiful. I miss you so much." I was still sobbing. "Your mother is dying and I don't know what to do without you. So many things have happened since you last held me. I just wish I could have kissed you, held you, told you I loved you just one more time. I did love you Blair with all my heart, and you broke it the day you had to go." I was on my knees crying at the base of the statue. I couldn't compose myself. I had never vented about it until now. I had never really spoken about how it made me feel, and the more I said the more I cried. "I miss you so much. You remembered my story about the garden and everything. You always did listen to me. I was blessed to have known you and if I could have given my life for you to go on I would have. All the money in the world couldn't replace you." I hadn't noticed the few spectators that had gathered behind me. "I just wish you could come back and hold me right now. Make love to me once more, talk to me in only the language you and I understand spoken by our bodies. I will always love you. Nothing and no one will take that away from you." I kissed the feet of the statue and rested my head at the base. It wasn't 'till I heard someone else's sniffles that I realized someone was watching me. I lifted my head to find that I was center stage. There were over a dozen people standing around the foyer in the hallways, in the windows. Nana walked over to me with tears in her eyes and picked me up from my low. She walked me over to that same chair, sat me down, and wiped my face. "You want to go back to your room?" She asked? "No. I'm fine. Just let me clean my face up some and I'll be right out." Nana grabbed my arm and walked me down the grand hallway and into a guest bathroom. She wet a cloth and continued where she left off only moments ago. "I didn't mean to cause a scene Nana." Despite the fact that I was apologizing, I wasn't the least bit embarrassed. I had something to say, so I said it. "It's all right!" Nana's voice was so soothing. "We all know how much you cared for him, and we all know how much he cared for you. Believe it or not though, you'll move on. You will! Your heart is hurting right now, I know, but if you keep it all in it builds up and breaks you like water through a damn." I listened to her words like the flowers listening to the sun. She rubbed my back as she spoke. I couldn't help but feel like she was doing me a service. It felt strange. Why was everyone on bended knees around me? I thanked Nana once more for her generosity and we proceeded to the garden. On the way there I asked Nana about Blair's mother. When was I to meet her? Where was she? Nana told me that I would be on my way to meet her in just a few moments. The house was magnificent. There were fresh plants everywhere, and they were most fragrant. If I'm not mistaken, there were marble floors throughout the rest of the house. Wood upstairs and marble down. Okay! We exited a large set of French doors and a whole new world unfolded before my eyes. There was a small little jungle back here. Nana instructed me to remove my shoes because the grass was really nice and all who step inside of this place have to be barefoot. Come to think about it, none of them had on any shoes. Wow. As we walked along the grass pathway there were even more flowers out there. They had a three feet Venus Fly Trap with a fence around it. The path opened up to a clearing where there was a pond and benches. There was also a pavilion to sit under with a barbecue grill. It was perfect. There were a whole bunch of people there. They had all stopped what they were doing to get a glimpse of me. Everyone turned around and they all watched. Nana pointed me toward another path though. She instructed me to keep walking and when I saw the door, to go in it, so I did. I walked for about five minutes or so until I saw a building. I wiped my feet and went in. A butler pointed me to a room and I went in. I opened the door to find a woman laying in a bed. I poked my head in. "Come in daughter." I did as commanded and went in. "Sit." The woman said. She was a cinnamon complexed woman with gray eyes and long brown hair that was braided around the crown of her head. "So, you are Simone. You are what drove me son's loins." I didn't know how to respond to that, so I didn't. I just waited to see what she was going to say next. "I am Nicolette. It's finally nice to meet you in person." Yes ma'am." I replied. "Please, I want you to call me mom, if you don't mind." I didn't mind at all, so I just nodded yes. "Guess you are wondering why you are here, well, you know why you're here, but not WHY!" I just nodded my head yes. "As you know Simone, I'm dying. I have a tumor about the size of a grape in my brain and it's inoperable. I still, until this time, didn't call you because I was fine. I've known about this for some months now, but now I know the end is near." She started coughing and a maid brought in some water. She ordered the maid and all others in the house to take their leave so it could just be her and I, and she continued to speak. "Did you love my son?" What! Did I love her son? "Yes, yes I DO love your son. I loved Blair since the first moment I laid eyes on him." I no longer felt nervous or shy. I could tell the world about Blair and now I damn sure could tell his mother. "Well, tell me about it." She said. I thought for a moment and decided that the beginning is always a good place to start. "I met Blair when I went out with a friend one night and he had my full attention. I gave myself to him that first night, and the things he did to me..., and the way he did them hasn't made me look back since. I would have given my life to keep his on this earth longer. I would have taken my life, if he asked it. He never had to ask for a thing and if he did he never had to ask twice." I answered her question with all my heart, and with tears in my eyes. I wasn't prepared for her next question though. "Ah, and what was your sex like?" What! I think I might have blushed a bit 'cause I was always put in my place when he was inside me, and I know I always made him feel like a man. "Uh, well,..", I paused for a moment. I didn't know what to say. There were no words to describe how he made me feel, what our love making was like, how it broke down every fiber of my being. "There are no words in any language, written or spoken, that can describe what our love making was like. It defies the laws of gravity and erases all space and time." With that said, she smiled. I told her our story from start to finish. I told her everything she wanted to know. Surprisingly she was all about detail, and found out why later. When Blair's father was around, he told Blair everything he knew about pleasing a woman. His mother said his father used to do the same things to her when they were intimate. I wish his father was alive now, I'd kiss that man's feet!! We continued to talk more and more about different things. Before I knew it I had spent the whole day in that room talking to her. Nicolette had dinner brought to us and everything.

Nicolette listened contently to every story I told her about Blair's and my experiences with each other. She asked if I had seen the statue in the foyer, and I told her about my little episode. It was a wonderful day. It was about eight o'clock and it was time for her meds and bed. I hugged and kissed her, and she told me to come back and see her tomorrow. It was dark as hell outside. All the tall trees hid the night sky from me for a second until I found my way back to that clearing. There were a bunch of different faces here now and a few of the ones from earlier. I could smell the weed from a mile away. That's one of the ways I found my way back toward the house. I sat down in a lawn chair. Armond appeared from within a crowd of people, all of which whom were staring at me. He parted the crowd and walked over to my position. He had a cup full of something with fruit in it and a huge blunt. I could smell his colon before he even reached me. Everyone was barefoot, which was cool, 'cause the grass was green and thick as carpet. The cool grass and the night air was a relief for this island heat. Everyone was a little shinny because of the thin layer of sweat that had gathered all over their faces. Armond handed me the drink and told me to relax. He put the weed to my face and asked me if I smoked. The answer to that question was a healthy inhale of the stimulating smoke. He passed it off to me and sat down beside me. "So how was it meeting Aunt Nicolette? I know she asked you a hundred and one questions!" I watched as the night seemed to compliment him in a way that certain notes complement a song. I let out the smoke and answered. "Yeah, she did. She wanted to know everything, so I told her everything. She's a great woman, and I wish I would have sat with her more before now." "Everyone is staring at you because they want to meet you as well. Blair was very well respected in this household, which is why they wait on you hand and foot." I looked across the clearing, and that's when I noticed that they looked like they were waiting for Armond to give them the "okay" to come over. "You are like a celebrity here. Get used to it. It'll be like this for a while." I nodded my head and they all came walking over. Some of the accents were so thick I thought it was another language and needed Armond to translate. We all sat outside talking and smoking 'till about one AM in the morning. Shortly after everyone started to disappear one by one, until it was just Armond and I. We talked and laughed almost until the sun came up. We both were high as kites, and drunk too. I don't know how we managed to stay up so late, but we were having a good time. We talked about work, and about the fourth time he told me to call him Simba, I got comfy with it. We talked about work and he was asking me things about the US and I was asking him about his travels through Europe. When I told him I was a scientist in the same field he liked to fell out his chair. Now, two high people talking about bio-chemical solutions and cellular decomposition is the funniest thing ever. We can barely keep our eyes open to speak to each other and we on some $E=MC^2$ stuff. I was cracking up about it, and when I told him about my realization he died laughing too. It was like we had known each other all our lives, like we were sitting back to back on a bench and never bothered to turn around until now. By the time we dozed off we were under the canopy. The weather was comfortable. I didn't need to cover up 'cause it wasn't cold, or take anything off because it wasn't hot. The thoughts of the day lulled me to sleep, along with Simba's colon, and as I slept that night I had a dream that I was flying above the night sky in Jamaica. I was just soaring through clouds and then into the ocean, where I swam next to whales and danced with mermaids and dolphins. I had a dream for once that I was happy. The next morning I awoke to a gentle nudge on my shoulder. Blair, I mean, Simba was gone. There was a light sheet thrown over me and there was some breakfast waiting on a tray in front of me. I felt refreshed and at ease. I looked around for Simba but he was nowhere to be found. The sun was bright and was hurting my eyes even though I was still under the canopy. Nana pulled the tray up the reclining lawn chair and proceeded to lay out the napkin in my lap. "What time is it?" It was sooo bright outside that I really couldn't tell what time of the day it was. "Ten thirty!" Nana said with a smile on her face. I was shocked when she said that. I had only went to sleep only moments ago but I felt like I had been sleep for years. I was up now but it was probably going to catch up with me later. Oh well. As usual the food was wonderful. Nana watched over me like a hawk. While I was in the house, Nana was never more than two steps behind me, or in front of me. Once more she sat and watched as I completed my meal without even breathing. She smiled at the pleasure of knowing that her food was being enjoyed. After breakfast I went to my room to take a shower to see Jamaica and all that it has to offer. After showering and cleaning up for the day, I decided to check my messages and e-mail. As usual there were like fifteen hundred calls from Weezy. I sat down at the computer and turned it on while dialing her number. "Girl what the hell is going on? Oh my goodness! Do you need me to come down there?" After I calmed her down so that I could get a word in edgewise, I told her I was sorry for not getting back to her sooner. "No I don't need you to come down here. And speaking about where somebody's been, where the hell were you at all night long? I must have called you a hundred times, and I even went and knocked on the door." I already knew the answer to my own question when she started laughing. Anything that keeps Weezy out of my reach really only has to do with three things. Work, family, and a man, and I knew which one of the three it was. I told her that I'd call her back after I settled things at the job. I was still not completely dressed though. I got in the shower, lotioned up with my favorite eucalyptus spearmint smoothing gel from Bath&Body Works and sat back down to the phone. I called into the office and everything was fine. Everything was running smoothly, and I instructed my assistant to email me all the results from testing so I could look them over, and I told her to keep up the good work and to call me if anything of any sort went wrong. I got off the phone with my assistant and sat back in the recliner. There was a wonderful view out the window and a lovely breeze. I was kind of turned on by the whole thing. I don't know if it was the air or all the weed I had smoked, but I was feeling real good. There was a bag of weed and rolling papers left in my room when I came in. It had to have been at least an ounce or so. I rolled a joint before I called Weezy. She was asking me a hundred and one questions, and to tell you the truth I had smoked too much weed that I was still high from the night before and I couldn't keep up. I told her to just take a breath in between each sentence. Weezy laughed at me. "Damn girl! I wish I had some of what you had, Simone. Girl, bring some of that back home." Weezy laughed. I hadn't fell back like this in such a long time. I couldn't remember the last time I felt this good. This was the best trip I had taken in a long time. I was by myself, and it was okay. Blair would be happy I was here. Weezy and I laughed, joked, and caught up for the next two hours. "Did you tell her about what's her name, Whyheeda?" "Hell no." I almost choked to death on the smoke when Weezy said that. I didn't even want to smoke anymore after she said that. I had to put it out. I looked down at the scare on my shoulder. It looked like lightning had reached out and kissed me. I thought it was kind of sexy though. It healed up quite nicely and the scarring wasn't that bad. I rubbed it like it helped me better remember the almost ending of my life. Weezy noticed that I had zoned out for a moment and brought me back to reality by screaming my name. "My bad. I was just thinking about it." I said, looking out the window. "Well!" Weezy said. "Are you going to tell her?" To tell the truth I hadn't really thought about it. Weezy always bringin' up some 'ol shit. "Damn it Weezy, I don't know. I really don't." "Nicolette was looking at the scare while we were talking but she didn't say anything. I'm sure it's going to come up soon though." That, even still, wasn't good enough for Weezy. "So what are you going to tell her?" I sat back and thought about it and said, "I'll just tell her I was struck by lightning." "Yeah, I guess." Weezy said. "I guess that bullet did come lightning fast!" We both fell out laughing at that statement. A few minutes after I hung up with Weezy. Looked up at the clock, it was almost one o'clock in the afternoon. There was a knock on the door, so I got up to answer it while I was still in my towel. It was Blair, I mean, Simba. "Hey Simone." The bass in his voice seemed to crawl up the hairs on my back, and pluck every note in my song. He wanted to know if I was interested in spending the day with him and taking in, "the wonderfulness of Jamaica," as he put it. I agreed and he told me to come down to the yard when I was ready. As he walked away I imagined him moving me with his body into the room and firmly removing my towel, placing those full lips around the dark circles around my nipples, sucking with the intention to remove my soul like milk. I just took a deep breath, hoping to catch the remains of his scent in the air, closed the door, and got dressed. Not long after, I was downstairs and ready to go. No sooner than I step out the door to the yard, there was a blunt placed in my hand from a relative I later found out was called Joe Joe, and he was cool. I can't remember Joe Joe not having some ganga in his mouth. He was a long beard, nappy dread. Joe Joe's dreads went down to his thighs. He wore it wrapped around the crown of his head when it was hot and would let them down in the evening. I took a few drags and walked over to Simba. He handed me an ice cold ginger beer and then we hit the road. After about fifteen minutes at eighty miles an hour, we wound up at this barbeque spot. I got some jerk ribs and he got some jerk chicken. It was soooo messy because of all the sauce, but it was so good! Everyone in the joint was licking their fingers. We talked about everything there was to talk about. We talked about how high we were the night before, and I told him about Nicolette, it was great! I was amazingly comfortable around him. It was like I had known him all my life, and could talk to him about anything. We ate and sat there talking for about two hours and hit the road once more. He wanted to take me cliff diving, and I wasn't too sure about that, but after some "pretty pleases", we went. I intended to go with him and watch him do it, but he wanted me to go off the hundred foot drop too. I didn't bring a bathing suit with me so we went to the "Irie" market place and got some swimming gear. The market place was full of culture. The smells, the colors, the people, all of it was going to my head. I was happy once more. Every few steps I took there was a dread trying to holla at me. I bought a piece of cocoa bread, some more ginger beer, and a few other items, and posted up at an old picnic table. The weather was gorgeous. I felt like the sun was kissing me, as if to say "welcome and enjoy." "So, what's in the bags?" Simba said sitting down. Simba's smile was so bright that it seemed to be life-giving, and I could feel from the day that I laid eyes on him that this was my second chance. We hung out at the marketplace a little while longer so our food could settle some more, and looked at some more of the items that the vendors so creatively presented. All of a sudden it started raining. This rain cloud came out of nowhere and started showering us with some of the warmest water. It really didn't matter at first 'cause we were about to go swimming, but then the drops got heavy and hard. We ran to the nearest awning for cover, but it was small and we had to stand close enough to where I could feel his breath on my neck. This shit was driving me crazy. I wanted him so badly, and the question wasn't if I should have him, but when? Just when I thought I couldn't take it anymore, the rain stopped. It stopped as quickly as it started. The sun came out and the air became thick with humidity. It had become hot now and our food was good and digested, so to the falls we went. We didn't talk much in the car, but it didn't feel odd at all. He put on the music, and I listened. We drove for what seemed like forever up into a trail. There was no place to change my clothes, so I just did it in the car. The woods were rich with all kinds of wildlife, and sounds. There were birds in the trees that I had only seen in magazines and on TV, and makes you wonder, 'is this a dream, and if it is, should I wake up?'. As we walked the trail I could tell we were getting closer and closer to the falls because of the slowly growing sound of crashing water. We arrived at a clearing that immediately made me think of the garden of Eden. The scenery was so perfect it looked like it was drawn. There were a few people out there, but not a lot. You could tell that this is one of the spots that if you didn't live here you wouldn't know about it. Not like the other sites that attract the tourists and such. It was really nice. Some folks had their personal grills out, and kids were playing in the shallow side of the falls. We stayed there until dark. A DJ came and set up, and started playing dancehall and slow reggae music. Later into the evening, all the children were gone and it was time for the adults. There were more people out here now as well, with big bonfires five feet tall for light. I don't know what it was, but it felt good, this feeling that I have. Simba and I ran around all night, splashing each other with water, eating and just enjoying ourselves. I met a few of his friends and a few of the family members from back at the house had shown up. Simba went and grabbed a blanket from the car, and we sat in front of the fire relaxing. "Simba, I'm glad I came here?" I confessed. "I know! Aren't the falls great?" He quickly replied. "No Simba, I mean I'm glad I came to Jamaica. I'm glad I was invited." Simba looked at me and smiled the smile of the gods, and that was all the response that was needed. "So when are you going back to see Nicolette?" "I don't know! Whenever she requests my presence again I guess! I don't know? I don't know what she wants of me. I sat and spoke with her a while when I went up there to see her, and I haven't heard anything about it since. I asked Nana, but she told me what I just told you, 'she'll see you when she's ready for me.', I don't get it." Simba takes a drag of a spliff he just rolled up and passes it to me. "I am so happy to be meeting all of you and I'm in love with Jamaica, but I can't help but feel like there is something someone's not telling me. Nicolette says she's dying, and that I had to get here before that happens, but so far I've spoken to the woman once since I've been here." "Simone, you haven't been here that long though. How long do you plan to stay?" He looked at me as if to say, 'no time soon.' "I'll stay as long as I'm needed, or as long as I can." It was getting late, so we got dressed and headed home. It was about ten o'clock, and we had been out there since about three. Plus, I got up early after being up all night, and I was ready to catch up on some long needed rest. The ride home was quiet and long, but I didn't mind one moment of it. We got back to the house and as soon as we pulled up Nana was at the door ushering us in. "How was you day sweetpea?" Nana asked. I told her about all the fun I had on the way to the room. As soon as I got into my room I just wanted to shower. I would have gotten in the bath but I might have drowned 'cause I was so tired. Nana helped get me out my clothes, as if I needed help, and set out some pajamas for me. Once I was settled in and Nana was sure that my needs had been met, Nana took her leave and bid me goodnight. After my shower I lotioned and lay on the bed in my towel. I didn't even make it to the night clothes Nana laid out. I turned off the light and lay still in the dark. My mind wondered for a moment straight to Simba. I haven't been with a man in five years. That is a long damn time, considering the fact that Blair and I would have sex round the clock. Huh, sometimes we'd meet for lunch just so we could fondle each other. But, as I lay there I couldn't help but to imagine how good it would feel to be next to Simba. How I would love to run my fingers through his locks and down his brawny back. I had, had a wonderful day and to have ended it with him inside me would have been the perfect ending. I also thought about Nicolette and why she hasn't requested to see me. This whole trip in fact was for her. "I'm going to go see her tomorrow," I thought to myself. The warm air gliding in my window blanketed me in my warm thoughts. Sometimes the wars that rage within us all too often have a simple solution, the difficulty in accepting the ending result whether we want to or not. It was there on that bed, in another country, under those stars that I faced my reality. I am in love with another man. I am in love with Simba. I awoke the next morning and after a few phone calls to work and to my mother I got straight into the shower and got dressed. I went downstairs and out to the yard where I had traveled the path to Nicolette. It was kind of early and I was still tired even, but I went anyway. I figured this would be better anyway so that there were no distractions from the other family members about anything. I went to the little house she was resting in and knocked ever so lightly and went in. As I concluded, she was awake. "Good morning child! What brings you out here so early." She said with a confused smile. "I just wanted to come out here and spend some time with you. I mean, that is why I came all this way." "Everyone wants me to see the sights moving me from one place to the other, I just want to see you." Nicolette smiled. She told me that she just wanted me to get out and see Jamaica, and that she didn't want me pinned up in the house. Nicolette rang a bell and ordered up some breakfast. We ate and chatted over breakfast. "You know, I am really glad you are here." Nicolette said. "I'm happy to be here, and I'll stay as long as you need me." Nicolette was quiet for a moment and then she looked away as tears began to fall down her face. I thought she was in need of her pain medication, 'cause from what I understand the headaches she got were enough to make the average person delusional. I proceeded to ring the bell for the butler but she stopped me. She reached her arms out and motioned me to sit by her side on the bed, and I went. "I miss my son." She began," I miss his smile and his laughter. I know I hadn't seen him in a while, but with all the pictures and the phone calls I felt like I was right there." She continued, "I remember his first steps and his first birthday party. I even remember the day he spoke his first words." While Nicolette was speaking, she was looking off into the distance out the window like she could see each moment playing on the sky line, and she began to speak once more. "But of all those memories, my favorite one is when he called to tell me he was in love and had met the woman he had planned to spend the rest of his life with. I had never heard my son full of so much emotion in all my life. Not when he graduated college, not when he got his first place, not even when he started his business. I hadn't heard such passion in my son's voice until he said your name. I was so looking forward to my grandchildren and their new beginnings, and when I spoke to you it was easy to see why you were the light of his life. I didn't even have to get to know you because for me, my son's word was enough, whole heartedly." I was now in tears right along with her. My heart was heavy 'cause Armond was my new cup of tea. How could I tell her what I was feeling for him? Blair's own flesh and blood! I couldn't help it though, it was like something I had never known before. I've got to tell her. What kind of woman would I be if I didn't. How could I look her in the face? "Yes it is true. I'm dying and I'm not really sure how long I have left, each day is a blessing. That is one of the reasons why you are here, but not entirely. There were some things that Blair didn't tell you and wanted to keep from you until you were married." Okay, what the hell is she talking about? What was he keeping for me all those years! I was on him like white on rice three hundred and sixty five days a year. Please don't tell me he had a kid or something over here. I wouldn't know what to do with myself. I sat back and braced myself for whatever bit of information that was to come to me. Nicolette sat back and smiled as if it were a load off her mind to say what she just said. "Simone, Blair came from a long line of countrymen. He lived the way he did in America because he wanted to, not because he had to. He wanted to earn his way through the world and be proud of the accomplishments he did himself, his greatest being you. Had Blair lived the life we wanted him to live he probably wouldn't have met you. "I always wanted my son to have the best of everything in life, and all he ever wanted was to live his life. He would have accepted his place here only if he had someone to share this with." Okay, she threw me for a loop! "All that you don't see and all that you do was to belong to Blair and his family at my passing. He is the heir to the Armstrong fortune. Our money has been passed down through many generations and Blair was next in line to receive it since he was the eldest son, but it is not set in stone. I can still pick whom I wish to take my place here." Whoa! I just sat there. I didn't know what to say. Was she going to say what I think she's going to say? Nicolette read the confusion on my face, but smiled and paid it no mind. "That statue of you was made for you when Blair told us he was going to propose to you, and it was to be a gift to you after you were married. The second part of that was you were to move here. He was going to bring you here and tell you the same thing I just told you. He was going to offer this life to you as your husband. Nana looked after Blair when he was a young boy and now she looks after you. We know everything about you, your likes and dislikes, favorite foods. This place was to be ready for the arrival of you. Just as Nana was to look after you and Blair, she was going to look after your children until Jah Jah chose to take her to his holy place. Simone, my son was a King." I couldn't move! I couldn't blink, I could talk. I just couldn't do anything. "Well," she said, "There have not been kings and queens in this country for hundreds of years, so I guess you can say we are more like a royal family, and I have made the decision to make you part of this family." She continued, "Simone, you will never have to worry about anything ever again and," Nicolette was talking and I got up to walk to the window. My mind went blank, and I could no longer think straight. I turned around and interrupted her speech. "You mean to tell me that Blair was royalty? Why didn't he tell me?" In a way I was mad. We never kept anything from each other, and now to find this out was like a low blow. Nicolette just looked at me and smiled. "Child would you have loved him any more or less?" I just shook my head no and looked out at the day light that was now early afternoon. I just wanted to kill myself, 'cause at least that way I wouldn't have to be haunted by Blair anymore and we could just be together in the afterlife. "Nicolette, what do you do when you've had the best? How do you settle for anything else?" Nicolette just smiled. "There is never just one great one Simone. Just like there were many great people throughout history. There is never just one, except for Jah Jah." I walked back to her bed side and I knelt down beside the bed. I wanted to tell her so bad about my feelings for Simba, but I couldn't bring myself to do it. I don't know what she would do. Hell, she'd probably put me on the first thing flying out of Jamaica so I remained silent.

This was just not the right time. I looked into her warm eyes as she placed a butter soft hand on my face and I said, "What is it that you are asking of me?" She leaned in and kissed my forehead, and that's when I noticed the sweat on her brow. It wasn't hot in the room at all, in fact it was quite comfortable, and that's when I knew something was wrong. It seemed as if she was gasping for air, so I stood and leaned her back into a comfortable position and proceeded to reach for the buzzer to call the butler, who also doubled as her doctor. Before I could even get within reach Nicolette grabbed my hand and told me to wait. I could tell she was in pain yet she didn't let out one sound. She pulled me close to her as I sat at the edge of the bed. I begged her to let me call the butler but she wouldn't let go of my hand. Now I know I'm strong enough to over power her, but I let her have her way nonetheless. "Simone," she managed to get out in between deep breaths, "I want you to take the place as lady of this household. I want you to continue the line of this family. I want the next generation to bare your roots." With those last words she was out. As soon as she loosened her grip I rang for the butler. He was there in a flash and checked her pulse and breathing, to which he concluded she had passed out, but in a deep sleep. The butler took something from a little vile with a syringe, injected it into her I-vee, and we quietly left the room. He showed me to the door and assured me that she was fine and that he'd take good care of her. I lay out in the hammock under the cool shade of the tree. I needed to get my thoughts together. Nana came out a few moments later to ask if I was in need of a meal on beverage. Moments later she returned with a small tub full of ice. Resting in the ice was a personal pitcher of guava juice, one bottle of ginger beer, and a pitcher of water. Nana rested her load on a small table, also hidden in the shade of the tree, and pulled a small plastic sandwich bag from her pocket and sat it down as well. I was in a daze. I began to feel things like I had never felt them before. The sun seemed to rest ever so gently on my lips. The birds were singing my favorite tunes, and the breeze appeared to be caressing me with its long fingers. My hallucination was interrupted by a tightly rolled Dutch, and a tall chilled glass of guava juice clutch firmly in Nana's hands, and heading in my direction. It wasn't even a blink of an eye, when I put it to my lips, that a struck match followed. I pulled a long and deep drag, and then slowly released it. Could I really do this for the rest of my life, alone? Could I stay here and live out the rest of my days lounging in the sun? They must have smelled the weed burnin', because not ten minutes later was the yard full of folks. Everyone had come out to join in the session, even Simba, who came out in a red tank and a pair of red linen pants that let me know everything about the kind of weight he was carrying below the belt, due to the fact that he had no underwear on. He walked right over to me, pulled up a chair and sat down. I looked at him like it was my first time seeing him as a different person. He knew the whole time. How long was he going to let me stay in the dark? Why am I so mad with him? He poured himself a glass of juice and lit fire to the healthy blunt in his hand, the whole time smiling at me. "Good day, beautiful!" He said. "Why the long face?" I exhaled and looked to the very beautiful Jamaica sky. "You knew didn't you?" He looked at me confused, like he was lost in the sauce, until I looked him in the eyes. "You knew the whole time. Did you plan on saying anything?" I slowly sat up and placed my attention on him. "No," Simba now looking at the sky, "I knew and was told not to say anything. Nicolette wanted to be the one to tell you, which I'm guessing she did." After a brief moment of silence, I took a nice long drag from the spliff, and reclined. "What did she say?" Simba asked. I told him about me going to see her without anyone knowing. I told him I did it that way 'cause I felt like I was under surveillance. He started laughing at me. "You were, you are!" I wasn't laughing. "We've had eyes on you since you got on the plane! We knew the moment you stepped out of the cab and walked into the airport." "I knew when you stopped for coffee, and when you sat down in your seat." I liked to fall out of the damn hammock.

"I was the one in charge of making sure your travel was as undisturbed as possible. I was the one designated to pick you up and bring you home. We've been preparing for your arrival for a long time." He turned and looked at me with a most excited look, like he was glad he could talk to me about it now. He continued. "You know what's funny? I was given a picture of you, but I didn't even have to look at it. The sun told me it was you when it kissed your face." His voice had gotten real soft, and so did his eyes. All I wanted to do was kiss him. All I could think about was kissing him! My lips wanted to meet his so badly that they started burning. Again he disrupted the silence, and got up and walked away. I had so many questions, and I wanted to chase after him, but the calm relaxing air bid me to stay put and let it hypnotize me, so I did. I sat for a little while more and retired to my room for a while. I looked at my phone. The incoming call box was full. There were a few different people wanting a few different things, but most of the calls were Weezy. "Oh lord, I'm gettin' ready to get cussed out." As soon as she picked up the phone she started screaming.

"Simone, if I have to come to Jamaica and kick yo' ass I will! What the hell are you doing? Are you okay? Are they washing you in chicken blood? I mean, talk to me!" I put the phone back up to my ear. "Hello Weezy." "Hello! Hello! Don't "hello" me!," she said. "Bitch you got me here worrying about you. You haven't been answering your phone or anything," she screamed. "Weezy, I just found out that I am the new heir to a family fortune, and if I accept it I won't be living in America anymore." With that bit of information Weezy had shut up. "Blair is of a royal bloodline and I was to be his wife. He had planned on moving me here to this absolutely to die for estate after we got married so we could spend the rest of our days here. But, now that he's gone his mother wants to leave everything to me, and not the other family members because Blair was heir to the throne, or whatever you want to call it. I don't know if I should start sleeping with one eye open, and to top it all off I am in love with his cousin!" Weezy was silent on the other line. I could tell from many years of knowing her that her jaw was on the floor. I don't know why I started crying, but I was. I've shed a little more tears this trip than I had really planned to. "Girl whoa, when did you find all this shit out?" "Today," I answered her. I gave her the whole rundown of everything that has happened since the last phone conversation we had. While I was talking to her I noticed that there weren't any phone calls from the office or the lab, so I checked my emails while we spoke. "Well, what are you going to do? Are you going to have him?" Weezy always gets to the meat and potatoes of things. "No! I mean, I don't know. I can't!" "And why the hell not?" Weezy stated as if she was scolding me. "Cause that's his cousin, and Nicolette might flip her wig. For hours I was telling her how when her son would enter the room my knees would get weak, and now I'm supposed to tell her that her nephew is in the running for doing the same thing! Hell no!" I was shaking my head, as if she could see me. "Simone, if Nicolette is really the woman you say she is, she'll understand. If she's really a woman, she'll understand." I just looked down at the floor. "Girl, I'ma tell you like this, you ain't really been with anyone in five years. That crazy bitch that shot you don't count. You let her eat your pussy one time, big whup! It's time for you to stop kidding yourself. Even Blair wants you to be happy!" Weezy had a point as always. "Girl Simone, if anything he's rollin' over in his grave 'cause his leaving messed you up." She was right. She was always right. Weezy was happy. Ronald is moving in and they're talking about getting married. I know I'ma be tore up at that wedding. I just laughed to myself at the thought of it. Weezy was right though. The only thing is that, I don't know if he feels the same way. No. No, I'm not going to say anything until there is a need to. Over the next few days I mostly stayed in the room. I sat back at the computer and caught up with the job. Everything was running smoothly back at the workplace. I spent the next three days on conference calls with my colleagues and staff. The development is going well. They were pleased with their conclusions and the data being produced from the testing. Barney, looking just like his name sounds, made this protype lighter to see how it would hold up with jet fuel in it! Needless to say it was a damn dumb idea. It took all the hair off his face. They told me he was fine and he wouldn't have to shave for a while. I just laughed, 'cause you do stupid things you get stupid outcomes. They emailed and faxed, I reviewed and signed. They told me to take my time coming back, there was no rush. "We're three months ahead of schedule." I looked at the phone like she was crazy. Sue and I are the beaker geeks. We do all the mixing. "Sue, how in the hell did you get fifteen thousand samples read!" "I guess I work too much!" Sue laughed. I was blown away. She must have lived in the lab for a while, which doesn't shock me. Sue was always the last one to leave work and the first one there. She's the type that stays in with one hundred and one cats, but her house is surprisingly clean. The staff goes over her house sometimes to drag her out for a drink. They had to do the same thing with me sometimes, but most of the time Weezy had everything under control. If she thought I needed a drink, she brought me a bottle. If she wanted me to get out the house, she'd tell me to meet her at one of our favorite spots, depending on the reason for the drinking. One night, around when I first met her, we got so drunk that we couldn't walk let-alone drive home, so we took a cab and gave him the wrong directions. We wound up skinny dipping in some guy's pool. He had a diving board and everything. The man came outside 'cause he heard the noise, and he was fine! I think his name was Andrew? Yeah, it was Andrew! He had on a pair of silk pajama pants on, that clearly let us know he wasn't wearing any underwear. Andrew was single and well off. He had a nice big house, and it was well furnished. Weezy and I jumped out the pool. We apologized and told him about how we were just trying to make the best of our "lost" situation. Andrew laughed and invited us in to dry ourselves and shower. Andrew wasn't built, but he had a nice body. His hair was tapered and it was red. He gave Weezy and I some sweats and we changed. Andrew was ready to call us a cab and Weezy blurted out, "We have to leave so soon." I was in shock! I choked on my water. We were still drunk but that was a sobering moment. She walked up to Andrew, and when I say she got in his personal space, I mean she stuck her hand down into those pajama pants to find the treasure inside. I was just sitting there with my mouth hanging wide open. "We don't have to leave just yet, do we Simone?" Weezy said. My amused expression was enough for her. I couldn't believe she was going to fuck him! Hey, but when you need it, you need it. Weezy gingerly rubbed his dragon, that was no doubt ready to breathe fire. Andrew looked at me, I looked at Weezy, she looked at him, he looked at her, she looked at me, and I just started laughing. This was the funniest shit since sliced bread. We were still done in by all the liquor we drank. I got up and walked over to Andrew, who was at a complete loss for words. Weezy is a bad bitty. She always had men throwing themselves at her, and she had a nice body! Poor Andrew's mouth was on the floor now. I walked over and rubbed his back and told him to relax. We were good. Weezy asked him where the bedroom was, and with "dragon" in hand led him there. I followed close behind. I was always up for a good show! Andrew's house was gorgeous. All I kept thinking was, 'I have to tell Blair about this place,' At the top of the steps we arrived at a pair of big white French doors, and I pushed them open. It was like walking into heaven. Everything was white. The carpet, the furniture, the linens, everything was white. I took a seat on the mini loveseat, that was in the perfect position to spectate. Weezy finally let him go and he walked over to a little box full of condoms. Weezy slowly slid down the pants and his penis popped up like a jack-in-a-box. It almost hit her in the face. He was bold. He had no hair on his dick. I was as clean as a baby's bottom. Weezy didn't hesitate to test its softness with her tongue. I think she liked the fact that it was clean shaved. On further inspection of the room, I noticed a big picture hanging on the wall behind me, and some DVD covers in a CD rack. Oh my god! This dude is a porn star. I just looked at Weezy and smiled. 'You hit the jackpot girl!', I thought to myself. Once they were both nude it got ugly in that room. He freaked the hell out of her. I came twice just from watching and rubbing my nipples. He put her legs over her head, flipped around backwards on her and all kinds of shit! I thought Blair and I had tricks up our sleeves, but we had nothing on the professionals. There were some things Blair and I couldn't do because he was too large. There were those special times where I would let him have his way with me, but then there were the times I was like, "Look dude, I have to "walk" into work in the morning." He would laugh and say, "No you don't, I'll carry you!" Andrew worked Weezy every which way but right! About two hours later we were in a cab on our way home. I had the dumbest grin on my face. Dru wanted to give Weezy his number, but she refused it and thanked him for giving her what she needed and we rolled out. Weezy is the shit. Andrew paid for the cab. He gave the musty Indian man a hundred dollars and told him to fly us back to whatever cloud we fell from. After a few moments in the cab I just started laughing. I knew from then on we'd be inseparable. I was going to know her for the rest of my natural and supernatural life. I had found my partner in crime. I went home that same night, took a shower, and woke Blair up so I could tell him all about it. It was like four AM. Blair rolled over and wrapped his arms around me while I told him the story. He was worried about us, and he was a little upset at first, not at the incident, but the fact that we were in a dangerous situation and harm could have come to us. I smiled and leaned into his ear and said ever so gently, "Was I in a dangerous situation when I went home with you that first night!" All he could do was smile. I started telling him what happened between Dru and Weez, and it turned me on. I started kissing him and rubbing him. It doesn't take much from me to get him aroused. Come to find out, he was hard when I got in the bed. He just wanted me to tell my story because it seemed important to me to tell him. Apparently that's why he was laying on his stomach.

Well, three weeks have gone by on the island of Jamaica, and I have loved every moment of it. We went four wheelin', and dirt bikin', and we swam in waterfalls. I was just having the best time. This is way better than the last vacation I was on. Weezy even shut down shop and made her way down with Ronald. They make a cute couple. They remind me of Blair and I. I love to watch the two of them together. One late night Weezy and I laid out in the yard. "This is the life Weezy. This is the life." "That's bullshit!" Weezy said. Well, I guess the Hypnotic was doing its number on her attitude. "What are you afraid of Simone, being happy for a change. Stop making yourself suffer. You're a good person, which is why good things come to you." My high just went away! "Simone look," and she got up and walked over to a cracked rock wall that overlooked the ocean on the far end of the yard. "Someone wants to give this to you, and what are you doing? Why are you questioning yourself? This belongs to you! I feel it, so I know you do too." I was at a loss, again, for words. "There is nothing wrong with you having the things you desire, Simone. You earned it, ….. you deserve it. There is a woman that is offering you something great, worth more than money. And there is a man that can fill that void that is overdue to be filled. Do you realize how many people would die to be where you are? It's okay to be happy. Would you deny yourself Blair if he came to you at this very second.?" "No!" I said so quickly I almost choked on my own spit. Weezy continued, "Then what do you think you're doing now? All of this is Blair! This land, that man, that dying woman, it is all him. He wanted you to have it." I just sat on the ground with my back against the wall and started to cry. She was right, as always. I love Weezy. "Forget about all that stuff back home. A house is just a house, home is where you make it. Doesn't this feel like home to you?" I just looked up at her and nodded yes. "Your family consists of a bunch of grown ass folks who can take care of themselves, and your mother and father would never have to want for anything. They could live out the rest of their days in peace and quiet." I just kept crying. "What do you want me to do Weezy! Yes, I'm afraid!" I stood up stumbling. "Yes! Yes I'm afraid to love something so hard and have it taken from me again!" I was mad now, but not at Weezy. I was mad at myself. "The world took him from me Weezy." It hurt so bad to say. The tears just streamed down my face. "How! How do I let go of the best thing in my life next to God, and oh yes he was a God to me! How do you let go of the greatest thing of all time, for the next best thing? Huh! How!" And before I could finish my breath Weezy hit me square in the jaw. I just stood there, looking at my own blood on my fingers. "That's how!" She said, "You fight!" "You fight the bad and the good, because sometimes too much good is bad." I was stuck. Every fiber of my being just halted in time, .. in space. I saw stars, I saw moons, I saw clouds, and I saw Junes. I laughed and I cried, I lived and I died. The earth moved slightly to the left, and I had an orgasm. I became hot, and then cold. I felt lost and confused, and then I felt secure and then found. For a moment I hated, but the feeling was quickly replaced by love. And then, that was it. I wanted to say something, I really wanted to speak, but it wouldn't come out, and before I knew it,….. there was another blow to my face, and down I went. The second punch hurt more than the first one. Now the pain set in, and tears began to fall. "Say something damit!" Weezy screamed! That bitch hit me hard as shit. Weezy wasn't a weakling! I met her at the gym, and we've worked out together for years so, when she hit me. . . it hurt. I just looked up at her with tears in my eyes. I slowly stood up now 'cause my buzz was completely gone, but she hit me hard enough to pause my motor skills, so that is what I had to recover from! I just looked at her while holding my mouth. "I don't know..", and before I could finish my sentence, she blurted out, "Simone, what do you want!" I went to speak once more and again she interrupted me, this time with tears in her eyes. "Simone, what do you want?" I started to cry harder, and so did she. Weezy took a step back and realized what she had just done. She looked at me and the mess I had become before her eyes, and took pity on me. Weezy could now see the twenty-four hour war I have been fighting in my mind since Blair died on my face. She saw through all the false smiles and all the unhappy laughter. All that was, was me. Bloody and beaten down by life's most common occurrence, death. I stood with all my insecurities and all my fears, doubts, and sorrows. I let them bleed out onto my face, my shirt, my skin. I let it run 'cause somewhere in this pain I felt pleasure. This felt,…it felt like a release. I lifted my eyes to the sky and let the moon intoxicate me. The smell of blood sat thick in the air. I focused my attention back onto Weezy, who was staring back at me. "Oh God Simone!" Weezy grabbed me, and yanked me toward her to hug me. She wrapped her arms around me tightly. "I'm sorry, …... I am so so sorry." Damn, Weezy beatin' on me now and shit! It was too much for me. Weezy was crying now like I had punched her in the mouth. I took a step back, without even looking at her, and stumbled to my room. The sun was coming up soon, and I damn sure wasn't ready to greet the day. I just walked with my head down all the way to my room, and shut the door. I got undressed and went into the bathroom to look at my face and make sure my damn nose wasn't broken. I threw the bloody clothes away and wiped off my face. I used a black washcloth 'cause I wasn't doing my own laundry and I didn't want the person doing it (Nana) to see the blood. I wiped my face off and rinsed my mouth out with some Listerine. That shit burned like hell! I didn't want to hit Weezy back until the stuff started to fry my mouth. But, I could tell she felt bad enough. She only wants me to be happy and I guess she's tired of me not truly being me and being by myself. If you know you're a good thing, why not share it with the world? God is all I need. He fills those places others here on earth can't. Next thing I know my thoughts into never land were interrupted by a knock on my door. It was either Weezy or Nana, and I didn't really want to be around either. I didn't feel like the questions and I didn't feel like the 'I'm sorrys' but, I went and answered anyway. I figured whoever it was knew I was up so I couldn't ignore the door, plus that's just rude. I walked my swollen nose and lip to the door and opened it without looking up, or even opening the door all the way. As I began to turn and walk away from the door, the breeze carried across my face a familiar scent. I stopped and looked up as I heard the door open behind me, and a deep voice from the darkness spoke in my direction. "Are you okay?" I turned around to see Simba in my doorway lightly blanketed by the night, as if to wear it like a silk robe. I looked down into his hand and saw that he was holding some ice in a towel. I looked back up at him. I was at a loss for words once more, and the tears began to fall once more. "I saw what happened, with you and your friend. I didn't want to come in between you." As manly as his physique was, his presence was as gentle as the brown tent in his eyes. As he spoke he walked toward me. "I didn't come down there because, what ever you and your friend were speaking about looked like it needed to be said." He smiled that ray of sunlight, and I felt warm in it. I was so tired at this point that I felt like my legs were going to give out from under me, and I began to sway, then poof! I was out cold. The last thing I remember is him reaching for me and the feeling of his hair across my lips, dreaming the dream of a thousand dreams.

    I slept really late into the day. I slept the sleep of the walking dead. The bed was so comfortable that all your worries went away when you laid in it. I feel like I'm on air every time I lay my body in it. When I woke up I didn't even want to get out of bed though. It was clear that my face was still swollen when I yawned and it felt like I had been hit in the nose all over again. I rolled over and looked out the window. That was one of my favorite things to do from this room. I just lay in bed for hours it seemed. I didn't come out to eat or anything. I guess Nana got worried about me, so she came up to the room. It was about seven thirty in the evening and I hadn't left the room not once. I just watched cartoons all day. I hadn't really turned the TV on much since I've been here, so I thought now was a good time to start. Nana came in with some home made stew that made my mouth water the moment the aroma touched my noise yet, I didn't move. Nana walked over to me and felt my head. When she saw my face her eyes got real big, as if she was watching the incident from last night unfold on my face. She stopped, paused, examined my face, and then departed from the room. Not moments later Nana was back. She had a bowl, and a rag, and some other stuff in unmarked bottles. I could see the steam coming from the water that I now knew was in the bowl. She sat all her little items on her trusty little table that she prepared everything on, for me. She gently tugged on my hand for me to come to the edge of the bed. Nana placed her bright white washcloth into the piping hot water, and let it soak. The washcloth was a bright bright white! You know, the type of white that glows in the dark. It was crisp and clean. I could smell the detergent on the fabric rising with the steam. Nana then grabbed a small glass jar that looked almost like a jar of Vicks. She removed some of the thick orange substance from the little jar and place it on every part of my face that was not in its usual character. It smelled like bat shit mixed with orange juice, and a hint of mint, which made me look at Nana like she had lost her mind, but I didn't say a word. She wasn't stingy with it either. She put a nice healthy layer of the bat shit on my face. I wanted to vomit and Nana knew it, that's why she was smiling. "I know it smells bad, but it'll feel good in a few seconds." Nana said, as she kept massaging it into my face. Once she was done with that, she took the rag out of the water. I know it was going to burn when she put that rag on me, 'cause the rag was steaming and it was eighty degrees. Nana placed the rag completely over my face. I prepared myself for the sting to my skin, but I felt nothing. She put the salve on my face so thick that all I could feel was the steam. It didn't even feel like it was directly on my skin. Nana told me not to move and let the concoction do the rest. It felt like my face began to vibrate. It felt like the ointment went straight to the sore spots and worked its magic. The warmer the rag became on my flesh the more the smell of mint filled the air. I began to relax, and once again, drift off into sleep. I lay there dreaming about Weezy and in the yard. I dreamt of that long walk to my room after that moment. My legs felt heavy for some reason, like I didn't want to go, but I didn't want to stay. I was looking at myself, looking at myself in the dream. I felt like I was floating now. I turned to see a light at the end of the tunnel, and it was a light so bright I thought that only God himself could shine that bright. I walked up to the man in the robe and kissed his feet. I kissed the hem of his garments, and the palm of his left hand. The man reached down and grabbed my face, and raised me to my feet. He kissed my face just under my left eye and next to my nose. There was a scent. Something oh so familiar, and I thought to myself, "Could this be real? Is the almighty himself in my mind?" It couldn't be though, 'cause there were not thoughts of love from a father to his daughter. But more like, from a husband to his wife. My eyes were closed, because for some reason I felt no need to open them. I felt safe, like this being was protecting me. Then I felt them, the softest lips in creation upon mine. I began to melt internally. It felt so real, like I was in my mind really experiencing this occurrence. I let out a moan as a hand caressed my nipples, and when it happened, I opened my eyes, it was Simba! Dream over. I jumped and sat up in the bed. The rag fell to my chest, and then slid down to my lap. As sure as I was that, that rag slid off me, I was sure that dream was real. And the first thing that came to my mind was, "Blair's trying to tell me something!" There has only been one time where I was kissed like that, and I got weak in the body. It was Blair with Simba's face! I know it. I got up and took off my shirt 'cause I was sweating bullets. I walked over to my favorite window and looked out at the night. On the way over there I caught a glimpse of the clock. It was eleven fifteen. Everyone was gone. We all hung out late, but there were still professionals that had to get to work. They lounge, but that's because they can. Almost everyone here owns their own business, in the medical field, or has something to do with law. When you sit back and think about it, there's a difference between being a bum just because, and being a bum because you earned it. We sit and smoke, and laugh, and eat, and chill. But, we also take care of business when it's time to, we exercise to keep our bodies fit, and we move and shake 'til sometimes we forget what it's like to sit still. I've earned my rights to this. I looked up at the bright star in the ski, that seemed for some reason to be smiling at me. "I don't know B. The last time I took a sign from you, some crazy bitch tried to kill me!" I laughed to myself and blew the star a kiss. "Well, I guess you didn't know the bitch was crazy huh?" Again I laughed to myself. "How do I know if this one is right?" No sooner than I said that, did that star shoot across the sky. "Well I be damned!" I winked at my run away star and went into the bathroom to wash that stuff off my face. When I turned on the light I was in shock! All the bruising had gone away, but there was still some slight swelling. After I cleaned up, and got over the shock of my face, I went downstairs to eat because I hadn't all day. I just made a small plate to heat up, and was on my way back to my room after I had heated it. While I was sitting there in the quiet, alone with my thoughts, in walks Weezy. "Whoa, you look like hell!" I said to her. She did though, and I couldn't figure out why. I was the one that got beat-up! "I didn't sleep so good last night, or what was left of it just before the sun came up." Weezy looked like she had beat herself up! I fixed her some ice cream, 'cause I know that's her favorite late-night snack. When I put the bowl down in front of her, she just broke out crying. "Simone I'm so sorry. I don't know what came over me. You are more than my best friend, you're my sister. Please say you forgive me!" And right after she said that, before she could inhale I said, "I forgave when it happened. I was just in shock, that's all! Weezy I'm good. Shit happens!" She jumped out her seat and gave a hug, and two best friends/sisters embraced for a moment. We sat there for a while talking. I told her how I came in the room and cleaned up, and how Simba came in with the ice and I passed out. I told her about the strange dream I had that rocked every nerve in my body, and I told her about the shooting star. Weezy laughed her ass off when I told her about that orange stuff, aka bat shit, that Nana had put on my face. "Bitch you hit hard as shit! I couldn't believe you hit me! Girl, I stepped outside my body so I could look at myself, that's how much shock I was in." We were both laughing. After a story or two more we called it a night 'cause Weezy looked like hell, and I could tell that she needed sleep. I just wandered around in the yard for a while listening to the night. I had some rum punch and called my mother. "Mommy, you sleep?" I asked in a quiet voice. "No baby. How are you?" In my mother's old age her voice had become soft and gentle. It was soothing and kind. Before I even knew what was coming out my mouth, I had told her everything. Weezy hitting me, me wanting Simba, Nicolette and her proposal, I told it all. My mother was silent, and so was I. I think we sat on the phone in complete silence for five minutes before my mother spoke again. I had said all I had to say, so all I could do was wait for a response. And out of all the things I had told my mother, the first thing she asks is, "Well, do you love him?" I was so far gone I had asked her who she was talking about! "Who mama?" "Simba! He sounds like he's a good man." I looked at the phone like my mother could see my face on the other end. "Mom, you mean to tell me that's the first thing that you can think of to ask me about after everything I've just told you?" I couldn't believe it. "Mama, what about my job? What about you and daddy? Moving to Jamaica, what about grandma, for goodness sake lady Weezy punched me, and all you can say is do you love him?" My mother started laughing. Her laugh was filled with joy and wisdom.

"My baby, the things you worry about are things that can be fixed and replaced. Simone, you are smart beyond your years and very well educated. There will always be a job out there for you, and as for dad and I, we'll be fine. We have been since you left home, and no matter what country you're in, we'll always be your parents. These things are all things that are an easy fix, but love, my baby, is something that takes more than a lifetime to get right. You were lucky to have found Blair when you did! You two spent some wonderful years together while he was here, and if he could live it again knowing he was going to die the same way he'd do it again just to be with you." My heart suddenly felt lighter. Mama always knew what to say. "Love is not something that's so easy to find. You can't apply for it, and contrary to what everyone thinks, you can't buy it either. There is something you see in that man that you saw in another man once before. You've been alone long enough baby. Life wasn't meant to be lived by yourself. You have to love someone who loves you back the same way. Only then will you be complete." The things she was saying were so real. Sometimes it was just good to listen, and this was one of those times. "Simone, you have everything material you could desire. You have money, a nice car, good job, and the only reason you don't have a house is because you don't want one. Do you know how many people want a house, but can't have one? You have something a lot of people don't have, Simone. You have choices. Baby, trust your needs, not your wants."

A few tears fell with my mother's last statement. I was restless and my mother was tired, so after a few more minutes on the phone, I bid her goodnight. I walked around for a little while longer. It was about three in the morning. I had messed my sleep schedule up sleeping all day, so I just went and did a few laps around the house until I worked up a good sweat, showered, and went to bed to try to fix my rest schedule back to normal. The next few days were wonderful. My face healed up just fine, and I had seen Nicolette a few times and she was doing good, and I ate and worked out, and went four wheeling with a few of the cousins on the beach. Weezy drove into the deep end of the river and got stuck, so we had to tow her out. She was mad, I was laughing! I thought things couldn't get any better. It was Friday night, four weeks after I first arrived. Everyone was going to the "Grassbar". It was like a club you could go to outside. It was a nice place to chill. They had food and wonderful music. They played live reggae and dancehall, and the drinks were strong and the air was thick with trees, and I'm not talking about the ones in the ground. The family would go any day between Thursday and Sunday. Everyone was getting ready to

THE NEXT BEST THING

go, even Weezy. I, on the other hand, just wanted to stay in tonight. After everyone left and the moon was high, I got dressed in some baggy blue jeans, timberland boots, my favorite red genuine leather belt with the scorpion in the buckle that I got for my twenty first birthday, a fresh wife beater, and my red bandana. I packed my book bag with some snacks, a blanket, pillow, cd player, and batteries. I went down to the shed where the four wheelers were kept, and took out the red and black one I usually drive. I strapped my cd case and sleeping bag onto the grill on the back, and ran back into the house to grab some off, a little bud, my wallet, and last but not least, my new fifty caliber satin nickel desert eagle pistol with drop holster for my leg. I let Nana know I'd be off the radar for a while, but that I'd have my cell phone. Nana told me to be careful and offered to make me something to eat for the long journey it looked like I was about to take. I kissed her forgiving cheek and ran out the door. I pulled out my mud kicker and fastened my face mask and goggles to my head, and started the engine. I had about a little over a half hour ride in front of me, and was going to enjoy every minute of it. My destination was one not so easily reached. The only way for you to get there was to take a land vehicle, and then you have to hike the last quarter mile. I was going to 'the lake of dreams' I called it. One day we all went four wheelin' and I got separated from everyone. I was lost for about ten minutes on the cruiser. I got off and walked to the top of the hillside thinking, maybe I could see something familiar up there. It seemed like a long way to the top, but I finally got there, and it was amazed. There was lush green forest, with colors so vibrant that they looked more real than life itself, like they jumped off the page of someone's imagination and right out into the world. There was a small rainbow within the clouds of mist that gathered at the foot along an elegant waterfall, maybe about a hundred feet up. The grass was thick and it looked like an emerald flat. The smell in the air was rich and sweet, 'cause the flowers were healthy in size and large in numbers. There were flowers of all colors, shapes, and sizes. The waterfall emptied into a large pool before traveling on to the ocean. It almost looked like this place was painted just as it was. There were birds playing in the ski, and I could swear that if I listened hard enough I could hear music. This place seems to caress all things gentle in spirit. It's that part of your mind you retreat to when the world becomes too chaotic to cope with. It's that place where even the bad weather is good, like the quiet before the storm, except there were no storms here, it's just the quiet. While I was there I ran down into the valley and took off my boots and socks, and stood barefoot in the grass. It was nice and cool. It tickled my feet and I began to laugh, and I just laughed until it hurt. I had been there for like twenty minutes by the time I had looked back down at my watch. I put my boots back on and climbed back up the hill. I knew they were about stir crazy by now worrying about me. I ran all the way back to the big wheel, which was fun 'cause it was downhill the whole way. I rolled the last twenty feet though 'cause I tripped over a tree root and went flying through the air. I was a little dirty, but no more than I was from riding, and no worse for the wear. As I placed myself in the seat I looked back up the hill side to the place that was nestled quietly on the other side, and vowed to return. I ran into the rest of the group in a clearing. We stopped for a moment, and they looked me over like you would a rent-a-car to inspect for damage. They asked about the bruise I had so recently acquired on my right shoulder, and I told them I had fallen off the four wheeler. I don't know, for some reason I didn't want to tell them what I had found. They probably knew it was there anyway. They know these lands like the back of their hand, they grew up here. I was happy inside when knowing I had found that place. Now tonight, for some reason, seemed like the perfect time to go. You know, while everyone was gone! I drove out into the night like a bat out of hell. Everything looked totally different at night time, especially when you're not really sure of where you're going anyway, but after a few times of getting lost I finally found the hill. I found a bush and after I locked up my wheels I packed everything on my back and began my hike up the hill. It took a little longer to get there than last time, and it was a little harder to climb the hill with all the stuff on my back. Damn near ready to fall over, I reached the top. I took a deep breath and went down into the valley. This place looked just as good in the blackness of the night. The moon shone through the waterfall and made it look like liquid crystal. It was bright, yet dark at the same time. I dropped all my traveling items and rested myself in the cool carpet like grass. After a moment, I gathered everything I had bought, and found a comfy spot on the edge of a platform away from the water. I wasn't a master camper or anything like that, but I do know that everything hangs out by the water, and to avoid any unwanted visitors in my tent I backed up a bit. I placed two four foot bamboo candles in the ground, and proceeded to build a fire. After I was done setting up house, I stood back and looked at my little setup. It was quite nice if I must say so myself. The pool of water was dark but the moon was my night light. I had placed rocks around in a circle to keep the fire from running around. I had found some sticks and started a nice healthy fire. I went to the water's edge and my reflection appeared clear as day. I looked at myself for a moment, and I smiled at the face looking back at me. I was older, but not weathered. I was wiser, but still learning life's lessons. My. . ., how the years fly. I've done some great things, although I wish I would have had some kids by now. I don't want my kids to have an old parent. I don't know though. You never know what the future brings, I thought. The water looked so inviting, and so I concluded that after a bit to eat, I was going to accept its invitation. I snacked on some salmon patties and rice that Nana had made for dinner the other night. I could eat them until I was blue in the face. I had heated it by sitting them on a flat small grill face that I placed on the stones, with the fire just below. The evening here was so seducing. After my meal I slowly undressed at the waterfront. I carefully took off each piece of my sweaty clothes. There were sounds in the night, but I didn't care. I was prepared to put a hole in "something's" ass if it came this way. I've had a gun license for years. Blair and I had gotten us some identical satin nickel .50 caliber desert eagle handguns, and yeah I knew how to use it. I kept it with me when I traveled. As I removed my socks and placed my feet in the lush green below me, I once again began to giggle because the grass tickled my feet. I am completely nude now but the air was so warm. If it weren't for the gentle breeze between my legs I wouldn't have even known I was naked. I walked into the water that, from playing in the sun all day, was as warm as a baby's bath. I reached down and grabbed the bar of soap I dropped just before I began to undress, walked into the water about waist deep, and waited for a minute to see if something was going to grab me. I would have run all the way back to the four wheeler butt naked if something had jumped on me! Once I was satisfied with the underwater surroundings, I swam over to the cliff side where the waterfall came down. I bathed and washed my hair in the naturalness of it all. I dove into the water and swam around playing like I was five years old; it was freeing. I climbed out of the water with a smile walking over to the tent. As I reached down to grab my towel I heard a branch snap. I stood still for a moment, not even standing up from the bent down position I was in. I reached over and grabbed the pistol and pulled the cocking lever back after taking it off safe. Once "thumper" was secured in my hand I slowly stood up. There was a good loom from the moon, but there was no telling what was lurking in the surrounding brush and behind the trees. I listen quietly for a moment more. Someone or something was definitely out in the night watching me, and it wasn't the mosquitoes. I heard some bushes wrestling then silence. All of a sudden out hops this big ass rabbit! I took a deep breath, and I would say I had to do an underwear check, but I wasn't wearing any. I relaxed for a brief moment, but once again I caught wind of a familiar smell in the breeze. I held the gun in my hand as I stood securing my towel around me," Simba? Is that you?" I said facing the darkness. I then heard footsteps coming straight for me through the shrubs. A large silhouette appeared slowly but surely in the dark, and then into the light. "Yes it's me", he said with his earth shattering baritone. "Don't shoot." He whispered, walking with his hands up as soon as he was sure I was able to see them. Remembering that the gun wasn't attached to my hand, I put it down. The smell of him invaded my senses like a robber in a secured home. It just took control of my mind, my movement. He walked up to me wearing an all black v-neck undershirt and black linen pants, that clearly let me know he wasn't again wearing any briefs underneath. Like so many times since this trip started, I was in shock. He walked up on me close enough to feel his body heat on my face. His pecs were at my eye level, and the loosely fitted undershirt let me know that his nipples had been found by the night's gentle breeze. It's funny how at this moment I felt like I was on fire. I was nervous and I had to control my breathing because I couldn't do anything about the beating of my heart, of which I could hear in my ears, and for as quiet as it was out here I was sure he could hear it too. "What,….. what are you doing here?", I slowly managed to get out. He stood in front of me like a mountain only God himself could move, and I stood in front of him like a deer caught in headlights, couldn't move. My mind kept telling me to take a step back, but it was like a magnetic force wouldn't let me, and my feet felt like they were weighted down. "I come here from time to time, to be alone and think." He responded faster than I asked. I then realized that there was water running down my leg, and it wasn't from swimming. I didn't look at him this entire time. I couldn't look into his face, and I didn't know what was going to happen if I did, and that scared me a little. "How long were you standing there?" I asked him. He smiled and revealed those ivory teeth, leaned over and said softly, "Longer than I care to admit." Everything around me seemed to stand still at this moment and my heart was beating louder, and bodily fluids were flowing so freely I thought if I took a step I would slip and fall. A set of warm hands grabbed my shoulders and pulled me close. Then a set of soft luscious lips kissed my forehead with endearment. The lips then went from my forehead to my cheek, from cheek to my neck, where they lingered for a moment. I let out a soft sight of pure ecstasy. The large warm hands then moved from my shoulders to the towel, and removed it exposing my erect nipples and trembling hot flesh. "What are you doing?" I said between moans. "What you want me to do." He responded. His fingers then found the moist center between my thighs and the sensitive flesh that was swollen and throbbing. His pants let me know he was more than excited and pleased by what he'd found there. I grabbed his massive arms for balance, because it was about all I could take. He gently rubbed me there in my soft center, and I couldn't control myself. I let go right there in the palm of his hand. Once I was able to ground my feet once more, he removed his fingers to sample what he milked from my body, sucking up every drop from his fingers, and then he kissed me. Everything stopped moving. The water stopped running, the wind stopped blowing, crickets stopped peeping, and my heart stopped beating. His lips felt soft as butter. And even though they were much bigger and fuller than mine, he didn't engulf my entire face. He gently sucked my bottom and upper lip, and let his tongue dance slowly with mine. After the kiss that seemed to take my life away in a moment, he took a step back. He lifted the undershirt up over his head and revealed a body that could have only been built by the world's greatest architects. Then, he pulled the string that was going to free him of his pants and they dropped to the ground. He was perfect. Not a scratch on him, like a brand new doll. Skin smooth, and soft as silk, he stood there in front of me naked. Simba stood there presenting himself to me, like as if to say, I'm here, this is me. Our naked bodies now stood two feet in front of each other. The trees began to sway, the water began to crackle, and the bugs began to sing like there was a force of nature about to occur. He reached for me and pressed his body to mine. The feeling of his bare flesh on mine was a feeling that I had long since forgotten. It just felt so good. He was rubbing me just right, kissing me every so softly, and touching me everywhere that drove me crazy. Though this was the first time I had ever touched this man, I felt like I'd been in his arms my whole life. He lifted me from the ground, cradling me, and carried me to the side of the fire that too seemed to await this outcome. He placed me in the sweet smelling grass, but instead of it tickling me, it caressed me. It was soft and fluffy, like a down comforter. He gently laid me on my back and took a place beside me. His erect penis lay across my right thigh as his fingers continued once more to explore my hidden places, and even though he kept his composer quite well, his dripping erection was a great indicator of what he was really feeling. It felt heavy on my leg and I knew I was in for a punishment from this ten pound, eight inch structure that he carried, but in a good way. He sucked on my nipples and toyed with my body for what seemed like forever because it was driving me mad. My body hadn't felt this way in years. I haven't been this moist and turned on since the night Blair asked me to marry him. We made love that night like we were going to die or something. Little did I know, he was going to. Tonight I was back on that fur rug in front of that fireplace, the same setting almost. Weird. When he couldn't take not being inside me any longer, I felt my little frame disappear under his massive body. He was so very careful not to hurt me. He was a very big man, yet he handled me like a mother would her baby. Every touch, strong, but gentle. He placed his lips on mine once again and slowly entered my world. It hurt a little, and I winced, but he held me close and kept his mouth on mine. He commanded me and relaxed me. He completely filled up every crevice inside of me. There was not even room for a thought after he entered me. It covered all sides and traveled all the way to the end. My bottom lip began to quiver and he moved me gently and smooth. My senses were so sensitive and everything around me just turned me on. The air, the grass, the fire, everything was seducing me. He moved inside of me but never moved himself away from my body. He massaged my core with his magic wand and it made me do all kinds of tricks. I was in complete ecstasy. My moaning was turning him on. The speed at which he pumped began to increase, and the sounds of my moans got louder and louder. His hips winded, twisted, and turned. The weight of his body on mine alone sent me through the roof. All of a sudden I felt hot. My mouth felt dry and sweat began to roll. I felt my body begin to shake. Yes, I was about to orgasm. He was giving me deep short steady strokes. His pelvic movements slid me up and down with ease. I felt my climax coming and his too. We were breathing heavy, and he moaned like a lion during feeding time. My screams bellowed into the night. There were animals watching, and stars shining on us. The wind tried to cool us, while the fire tried to warm us. I looked up into the black star littered ski. My toes curled, and my life with Blair flashed before my eyes. My body rose from the earth. My teeth embedded in Simba's chest, but he didn't seem to notice at all. He was so strong. I cried out with my body shaking under him. He was holding me tight because his release was following mine. That moment in front of the fireplace was again relived. As my breathing began to return to normal, and my muscles relaxed, the tears began to flow, I cried softly to myself. Simba rested himself on me breathing heavily as well. His orgasm also appeared to be a big one. Our bodies shaking with after-glow, he looked in my eyes. He wiped the tears from my face and said, "Did I hurt you my love?" I shook my head no, and he kissed my forehead. He wiped a tear from my eye and smiled at me. I smiled back. We lay outside by the fire for a while more. The air was just right so we didn't need to cover because of cold. I lay on top of him resting, feeling like I was suspended in mid air. I lay there looking at the fire and out into the night as he rubbed my back ever so gently. I was happy again inside. Not only because I was going to start a new chapter of love in my life, but because…I was going to get to do it again with my love.

www.ingramcontent.com/pod-product-compliance
Lightning Source LLC
LaVergne TN
LVHW041847070526
838199LV00045BA/1472